"My life is over.

"I only just fully realized it. The Mafia hit on me won't ever expire. It'll just run and run until I'm found. And then someone will pocket two million dollars and I'll be dead," Goldie said quietly.

Zeke wasn't sure what to say. It was true that most people caught in the crosshairs of the Mafia disappeared, either into the witness-protection program or a shallow grave.

"The FBI can help you," he said, going to sit next to her. "They'll relocate you, give you a new life. You'll be safe."

She stood, bathed in the light of the overhead bulb, her hair shining like copper wire, lustrous and glossy. But something else was glinting on her head, something red and skittish, a dot that bounced across her hair and came to rest on her forehead.

"Goldie!" he yelled, springing from the couch. "Get down."

Elisabeth Rees was raised in the Welsh town of Hay-on-Wye, where her father was the parish vicar. She attended Cardiff University and gained a degree in politics. After meeting her husband, they moved to the wild rolling hills of Carmarthenshire, and Elisabeth took up writing. She is now a full-time wife, mother and author. Find out more about Elisabeth at elisabethrees.com.

HUNTED BY THE MOB

ELISABETH REES

LOVE INSPIRED SUSPENSE
INSPIRATIONAL ROMANCE

LOVE INSPIRED® SUSPENSE
INSPIRATIONAL ROMANCE

ISBN-13: 978-1-335-72182-2

Recycling programs
for this product may
not exist in your area.

Hunted by the Mob

This edition published by arrangement with Harlequin Books S.A.

For questions and comments about the quality of this book, please contact us at CustomerService@Harlequin.com.

Love Inspired
22 Adelaide St. West, 40th Floor
Toronto, Ontario M5H 4E3, Canada
www.Harlequin.com

Printed in U.S.A.

Come unto me, all ye that labour and are heavy laden, and I will give you rest.

–Matthew 11:28

For my wonderful friend Suzanne,
a woman of pure and steadfast faith.

ONE

The heat of summer hung in the air, moist and heavy under a midday sun. Agent Goldie Simmons stepped from her vehicle into the humidity, wishing she had worn something other than jeans and sneakers that day. Standing in the driveway of a beautiful stone mansion in the exclusive suburb of Gladwyne, Pennsylvania, she could smell chlorine from a pool in the backyard and closed her eyes to imagine slipping into the freshness of clear water.

"Oh boy," she muttered to herself. "This assignment might be my best one yet."

Retrieving her case from the trunk, she waved at a female police officer standing guard at the front door of the palatial home.

"You must be Agent Simmons," the officer called. "I was told to expect you and you're right on time."

Goldie laughed. "I have many flaws, but

time management is not one of them." Wheeling her suitcase along the path, she held up her ID badge for the officer to scrutinize. "Did my partner, David McQueen, arrive already?"

"Yes, ma'am. He got here two hours ago."

Goldie read the name tag attached to the woman's shirt. "You look a little hot, Officer Diaz. I hope you're keeping hydrated."

The officer smiled. "Actually, ma'am, I could do with some water. The force doesn't supply us with a bottle, and I've been on guard duty for three hours without a drink."

"That's not right," Goldie said, shielding her eyes against the blazing sun. "Come inside and get some water."

"I'd appreciate that. The house is so secure. It's kept locked at all times. This place is like Fort Knox."

Goldie retrieved a key, which she'd been issued beforehand, from her jeans pocket. "It's no surprise that this house is on lockdown, right? The lady who lives here has the power to bring down one of the biggest Mafia families in America."

Mrs. Louisa Volto was the wife of the infamous Leonardo Volto, a ruthless Mafia boss, who, alongside his brother, Joseph, was facing multiple criminal charges, ranging from money laundering to murder. Mrs. Volto had cut a deal with the prosecutor in exchange for immunity and a sizable chunk of assets, but that betrayal had put her in potential danger. Despite being seven months pregnant with her husband's child, she was still a potential target, the star witness in a trial currently taking place in a Philadelphia courthouse where she was due to give her testimony in just two days.

Goldie unlocked the door and entered the wonderfully cool interior where polished floors, large paintings and an aroma of lilies reminded her of an upmarket art gallery. Officer Diaz followed her inside and Goldie locked the door behind them and pocketed the key. "It's quiet in here, huh?"

"Yes, ma'am. I guess Mrs. Volto is resting, what with being pregnant in this awful heat."

Goldie walked along the wooden boards in the hallway, a faint scent of polish rising to her nose. This home was remarkable, likely more than one hundred years old but perhaps still as beautiful as the day it was built, with many of its original features well preserved.

"I'll go find David while you get yourself a drink," she said, admiring the intricate molding on the high ceiling. The kitchen was clearly visible directly ahead, so she pointed the way. "There's bound to be some ice in the freezer to cool you down."

"Thank you, ma'am."

As the officer left her side, Goldie walked through the living room and raised her eyebrows at the overt display of wealth. Sculptures, gilded mirrors, vast white sofas and Persian rugs all combined to create an opulence that she had never seen before. Coming from a dirt-poor and unhappy childhood home, luxury was completely alien to Goldie, and she could only imagine the kind of privilege that Mrs. Volto's baby would soon be born into.

Hearing Officer Diaz running the faucet in the kitchen, she continued her tour of the first floor, noticing an open door to the patio out back and heading that way. Just as she stepped onto the brightly colored tiles, she stopped in her tracks. A man was standing next to the pool, his back to her, staring over the endless rolling hills beyond the perimeter fence. He wore a Hawaiian shirt and boat shoes, one hand in the pocket of his beige shorts, the other casually resting on the handle of a holstered gun. With his mousy blond, tousled hair and olive-toned skin, this certainly wasn't David McQueen, her FBI partner of eight years. And with no sign of

David, or of Mrs. Volto, this stranger's presence could only mean one thing: danger.

Without a second to lose, she ran hard toward him, dropping her gun to the ground before knocking into his upright figure like a bowling pin, sending them both crashing into the pool. The effect was a little like being in a washing machine, spinning below the waterline, uncertain of which way was up. Goldie saw the man's gun slip from its holster as he thrashed in the water, and she felt a sense of satisfaction watching the weapon glide to the bottom of the pool. She then broke through the surface right at the edge and grabbed her own weapon from the ground. But when she tried to pull herself out of the water, her jeans and sneakers were too heavy, weighing her down, and she repeatedly slid back into the pool with a splash. Instead, she held her gun above the water, waiting for the guy to emerge, and when he did, he was spluttering and coughing, rubbing the chlorine from his eyes.

"I'm an FBI agent and you're under arrest," she said, desperately trying to tread water and maintain control of her weapon. "Swim for the steps and get out slowly."

The man stared at her in confusion, watching her struggle. For a good few seconds he said nothing, narrowing his eyes, running his gaze across every part of her face.

"Marigold?" he said finally. "Is that really you?"

She kept her gun aloft, heart hammering. Nobody called her Marigold anymore. She'd left that old life behind. "Who wants to know?"

The man pushed his mousy hair from his forehead. "It's me, Ezekiel. How long has it been? Twenty years at least."

"Zeke?" She could scarcely believe it. "You gotta be kidding me."

Could this tall, beefy man really be Ezekiel Miller, the sweet boy she'd once thought she'd marry when she was just seventeen years old? The same boy who'd promised to whisk her away from her horrible home life? The boy who refused to answer her letters and did nothing to try to find her when her father suddenly moved their entire family from the small town of Glenside, Pennsylvania, to Ohio after he'd been discovered embezzling money from his accounting firm to pay his gambling debts?

"What are you doing here?" she asked, finally beginning to recognize his features, the way his eyes seemed to disappear into slits when he smiled. "This house is off-limits to civilians. Strictly law enforcement only. I could've shot you."

Breathless with exertion, she clung to the edge of the pool, gun still in her hand, taking no chances with this man she'd once loved with her entire being. Having been part of the same church since babyhood, Goldie and Zeke had grown up together, forming such a tight bond that they were often referred to as "Ezigold." But just like God, Zeke had abandoned her when she needed him the most.

"I *am* law enforcement, Marigold," he said, hauling himself onto the steps and reaching into his pocket to pull out an ID badge. "I'm with the Bureau in New York. They sent me here to cover for an agent whose wife went into early labor last night. Since I know Philly pretty well, they thought I'd be a good fit."

Goldie's partner's wife, Lilly, was due to give birth in three weeks, but Goldie had no idea the baby had decided to make an early appearance. Nobody had told her.

Zeke clearly noticed her concerned expression. "Everything's okay," he reassured her. "David left a message on your cell when you didn't pick up. The baby was born this morning. It's a boy."

"I noticed a missed call from him, but I didn't think it was important." David was something of a stickler for detail and often called to discuss minor points of a case. "He's got a baby boy, huh? That's great."

But try as she might, Goldie simply couldn't bring herself to feel the level of joy that should accompany news of a healthy newborn baby. All she could think about was Zeke and how on earth she was going to handle her sudden and jumbled mess of emotions.

"Here," he said, wading into the water to extend a hand. "Let me help you out. You look a little shell-shocked."

She took his hand and allowed him to pull her onto the graduated steps, where she stood with shaking legs. "I have so many questions right now, Zeke," she said. "You are the last person I expected to see today." She shook her head, wringing out the water from her long red curls. "Why did Officer Diaz tell me that David was here? She must've looked at your ID, surely?"

Zeke frowned. "Yes, *he* checked my ID thoroughly. Officer Diaz is a man."

"What are you talking about? I met her a couple minutes ago. She's petite with dark hair and…" She stopped, slapped a hand to her forehead. "Oh no! No, no, no. I let her into the house to get a drink of water."

The shakiness in her legs dissipated in an

instant as she leaped from the steps and onto the warm patio tiles. If Officer Diaz was a man, then exactly who was the woman Goldie had just admitted into the house?

"We have to find Mrs. Volto," Zeke said, running toward the house, leaving his weapon on the bottom of the pool. "If she's in danger, you'll have to do the shooting."

All thoughts of Zeke's abrupt and shocking return to her life now had to be put aside. He was her partner for this assignment and whatever history they shared had to be forgotten, or at least buried deep. Goldie was a professional adult now, not a scared teenager who desperately needed Zeke's support and reassuring arms around her. She was a strong and capable person.

Following his wet footprints through the patio door, she made a grab for his elbow and put a finger to her lips, encouraging him to stop and listen for a moment. From upstairs came the sounds of voices, raised and angry. Then a heavy thud sounded on the floor and a woman cried out, "No!"

Both agents went into immediate action, tearing toward the stairs and vaulting them two at a time. A specially built panic room had been installed in a corner of the upstairs hallway, but Mrs. Volto had clearly not been able to take advantage of it. The steel door was open, the reinforced chamber empty.

"Here," Zeke called, pointing to a door that Goldie guessed must lead to Mrs. Volto's bedroom.

With a swift kick from Zeke's foot, the door flew open to reveal Mrs. Volto on the floor of her lavish bedroom, bleeding from a cut to her lip and clutching her belly. Meanwhile, the phony Officer Diaz was standing over her with a heavy, crystal vase in her hand, an expression of absolute hatred on her face.

"Stop right there!" Goldie held her gun aloft. "Back away and put the vase on the floor. Slowly."

The woman's eyes snapped up and locked on to Goldie's as her chest rose and fell with her rapid breathing. She was highly agitated, by the look of it.

"Please, Marsha," Mrs. Volto said in a pleading tone. "Please do as she says."

Goldie inched her way into the room, dripping pool water onto the carpet, Zeke right behind her. "Do you know this person, Mrs. Volto?" she asked.

"This is Marsha Volto, my sister-in-law. She's married to my husband's brother, Joseph."

Goldie skirted to the side of the room to get

a better vantage point, her aim as steady as a rock. "Don't make me shoot you, Marsha," she said, addressing the suspect directly. "I don't want to do that. You gotta back off."

But Marsha stubbornly maintained her position, the crystal vase held high over Mrs. Volto's head. As she was still in her fake uniform, there was a gun holstered at her waist, and Goldie wondered why Marsha hadn't used it already. Was there a more personal score to settle here?

"Think of the baby, Marsha," Zeke said gently, pointing to Mrs. Volto's stomach. "That's your niece or nephew in there, right? They're innocent in all of this."

Marsha narrowed her eyes at Mrs. Volto. "You deserve to die for what you've done, Louisa," she spat. "The family trusted you and you betrayed us." Her voice rose to a screech. "You're a dirty, rotten liar."

She lifted the vase even higher, and Mrs. Volto suddenly turned toward Marsha and kicked out with her foot, making contact with her attacker's knee. Marsha lost her footing and dropped the vase onto the deep-pile carpet, making a grab for her gun. Goldie yelled out a final warning, but as Marsha yanked her gun from its holster, she was forced into immediate action. She fired her weapon.

As the sound of the bullet reverberated in the air, Marsha crumpled to the floor, blood oozing from a bullet hole in her chest. Zeke sprang forward, pulling a folded towel from the dresser to press onto the wound and stem the flow.

"You go see to Mrs. Volto," he said. "And call for backup."

Goldie holstered her weapon, pulled out her radio and made a request for an emergency response team. Then she knelt next to Mrs. Volto and put a hand on her shoulder.

"Medical help is on the way," she said soothingly. "Is the baby okay?"

Mrs. Volto sat up and placed her arms around her stomach protectively. "Everything is fine, and I can feel the baby moving." She looked across at Zeke desperately working to prevent the injured woman from bleeding out. "How is Marsha?"

Zeke's expression was contorted into a grimace, his fingers splayed and pressed onto the towel, now saturated crimson. "I can't stop the bleeding." He placed two fingers on Marsha's neck as she lay supine on the carpet and rested them there for what felt like an age before shaking his head. "She's gone."

Goldie's shoulders slumped. Taking a life was never an easy decision and caused her a huge amount of pain, even when she had been given no choice.

Zeke stood, lifted a clean bath towel from the dresser and shook it out to place over the body. He then knelt on the carpet, laced his fingers and looked across at Goldie. "You want to join me in a prayer?"

She jumped to her feet. "Really, Zeke? You think that'll solve anything?"

His brow wrinkled. "It won't bring her back, but whatever wrong she did in her life, we should ask God to have mercy on her now that she's passed."

Goldie rolled her eyes. She had battled with a fragile faith throughout her twenties, but some years ago it had shattered into teeny, tiny pieces, and Zeke's legacy had played a big part in its breaking. He was the first person to prove to her that belief meant nothing, that prayer was pointless. She had asked God to help her a million times over, to show her the way back to Zeke. And now it was too late. She was too old, too cynical and too distrustful to care anymore.

"I'll pray with you," Mrs. Volto said, shuffling across the floor.

"You two can pray if you like," Goldie said, heading for the door. "I'll go wait outside for backup to arrive."

"Marigold," Zeke called. "What happened to you? You always said your faith was unbreakable."

She turned. "I'm called Goldie these days, Zeke. And guess what—I grew up over these last twenty-one years. Maybe you should try it."

With that, she strode from the room, brushing away a tear as she went.

Standing in the doorway of the kitchen, Zeke stole numerous glances at Marigold as she sat at the table giving a statement to Karl Bauer, the special agent in charge of this protection assignment. Zeke's childhood sweetheart had barely changed in twenty-one years. Her long, tightly curled hair was exactly the same color as it used to be, as coppery and vibrant as a sunset. And her freckles hadn't faded on her cheeks, nor had her green eyes lost their ability to set his heart beating. But something had clearly changed inside her character. She was cynical and tough, having built a high internal wall. There was no way she wanted to be friends, that was for sure. And considering her prickly nature, friendship wasn't on his agenda, either.

She glanced his way, locked eyes with him and held his gaze, defiant and fierce.

He wasn't sure what he'd done to deserve this kind of hostility, because Marigold herself was the one who'd cut contact all those years ago.

Her family had vanished from their Glenside home out of the blue one day, right after rumors started to circulate about her father's gambling addiction and suspected embezzlement from his employer. Zeke, of course, had always known that Mr. Simmons was a gambler and a liar and cruel with his words. Marigold had confided all of these secrets to him, leaning on him and building up a powerful relationship. Despite being only seventeen, they knew they were in love, destined to marry one day. Or, at least, that's what he'd assumed.

Goldie had made no attempt to contact him once she'd moved away, and he gave up hope of seeing her again after graduating high school. When his parents made the decision to relocate to New York, he'd decided to make a fresh start and put the memory of Marigold behind him. But no matter how hard he'd tried, he had never gotten over losing her.

"What I don't understand," he heard her say to Karl, "is why Marsha didn't just shoot Mrs. Volto immediately. If her goal was to eliminate the trial's star witness, a bullet would've done the job far quicker than a crystal vase. She had a loaded gun right there on her hip."

"I agree," Zeke said, moving closer. "What we saw between Louisa and Marsha Volto was personal. Marsha was really mad."

"Of course she was mad," Karl said incredulously. "Louisa Volto has done the worst thing possible in Mafia circles. She ratted out the family."

"I think there's more to it than that," Zeke said. "Marsha was in Louisa's bedroom for at least four or five minutes before we realized what was going on. What did they talk about for that length of time?"

"I don't know, because Louisa is too traumatized to give me a statement," Karl replied, rubbing his stubbly bald head. "But our undercover Mafia sources indicate that Leonardo Volto didn't order the attack. He's so far refused to place a hit on Louisa while she's carrying his unborn child, so it looks like Marsha was acting alone. It just goes to show why this protection detail is badly needed. There might be plenty more lone wolves in the Volto family who are happy to go against Leonardo's wishes."

"That's a certainty," Zeke said. "But Marsha wasn't a lone wolf, was she? I hear that the real Officer Diaz was found bound and gagged in the garage and she can't have done that all by herself, can she? What has Diaz been able to tell us?"

"He says it all happened very quickly," Karl replied. "He was checking a noise in a hedge when a bag was placed over his head and he was manhandled into the garage, where he was tied up and his shirt removed. You're right—Marsha must've had help to do that, perhaps a friend of her husband's. If Marsha manages to eliminate Louisa, then her husband most likely walks free."

"Well, her plan worked perfectly, because she got inside with ease," Zeke said, avoiding Goldie's eye. "But then she totally messed up. She had an ideal opportunity to murder Louisa and get out of the house quickly, but she wasted time by getting into an argument. Why?"

Karl shrugged. "People do strange things when they're driven by anger, and we're incredibly fortunate that Marsha wasn't thinking straight, because we almost lost our star witness today, not to mention her innocent baby." He eyed them both. "I do not want this kind of scenario to happen again. I hope you two understand that I expect you to tighten up your security protocols."

They answered in unison. "Yes, sir."

"I've also noticed a little animosity between you," Karl said ominously. "And I don't care to know the details, but you'll need to cooperate and share your expertise in order to complete this assignment successfully. Don't let me down on this."

"No, sir."

He rose from the table, gathering his paperwork. "I'll go try to coax a statement out of Louisa. She's terrified, and I'm concerned she may try to back out of our deal." He rubbed a hand across his scalp again. "This is turning into a very bad day."

As soon as Karl left the room, Zeke took his empty seat and placed his hands on the table, fingers twined. "Listen, Marigold…" he began.

"I already told you, Zeke," she said, giving him a look of scorn. "It's Goldie now."

"Right, of course." He smiled. "Old habits die hard, I guess."

"Except the old habit of loving me, huh?" she shot at him. "You let *that* die pretty easily from what I remember."

"What are you talking about?" he said disbelievingly. "I never stopped loving you, not until I realized you weren't coming back. You never even said goodbye."

"My dad wouldn't let me come see you before he drove us all to Ohio in the middle of the night," she said, her voice creeping higher. "He told us to cut contact with everybody in Glenside, but I wrote you letters in secret. And you ignored every single one of them."

"Letters?" He cast his mind back to those dark months after Goldie's family had vanished. "I never got any letters."

She searched his face. "Well, I sure sent them, ten in total. And I called your house a bunch of times but I just got a message that the number was disconnected. It seemed like you were trying to erase me from your life." She raked her fingers through her red curls. "I can't believe I'm still hurt about this even after twenty-one years. I must be crazy."

"You're not crazy," Zeke said. "You have every right to be hurt, but I promise you that I didn't receive any of your letters." Still searching his memory, he was reminded of things his parents had told him at the time. "Not long after you left, my dad said we needed to change our telephone number because of some crank calls." Now he started to see things with more clarity. "And when he saw how much I missed you, he told me to move on. It's possible that he also destroyed your letters before I got to see them."

Goldie's mouth dropped open. "Why would he do that?"

How honest should he be with her? At one time he would've told her everything, trusted her to react with calmness and maturity, but now he wasn't so sure.

"When my parents found out what a devious person your father was, they were horrified that he'd been lying to the church for years, and they said they never wanted to see his family in Glenside again."

"And that includes me too, right?" she challenged.

"They never said it outright, but I guess so."

She folded her arms. "I'm not overly surprised. That's the kind of behavior I've come to expect from good Christian folks."

"That's mean." Deep down, he knew she had a valid point, but he was on the defensive. "They were doing what they thought was best for me."

"What about what was best for me, Zeke?" she said, standing up abruptly. "Everything changed overnight for me. I was put in a new school where I had zero friends, and I wasn't allowed to talk about our old life because there was a warrant out for my father's arrest." She let out a laugh. "We joined a new church in Cleveland, you know that? Dad continued to hide behind a veneer of respectability, pretending that he was a pillar of the community."

His heart heaved for her, for the innocence she had lost.

"What happened to him?" he asked.

"The police finally caught up with him after about a year, and he was sentenced to twelve years in federal prison for embezzlement and tax evasion. My mom lost our apartment, our car, just about everything, and we could barely put food on the table. Right after I graduated high school, I joined the army and started supporting her and my sister. Nobody else would help us."

"Oh Goldie," he said, standing up to hold out his arms and invite her to take comfort in a hug, but she remained motionless. "If only I'd known where you were, I'd have come see you and tried to help. I'd never have left you to deal with all of that on your own."

"I went to your home in Glenside when I finally saved up enough money for the bus ticket," she said. "I thought I'd try one last time to see you before heading off to the military base, but a new family was in your house. They said you'd moved to New York."

She bit her lip, steadied her breathing. "It was then I knew I'd never see you again."

He smiled weakly, letting his arms drop to his sides. "But here I am, huh?"

"Yeah," she said, not returning his smile. "Here you are."

She was apparently building her wall even higher.

"I'm sad that things turned out this way, Goldie," he said. "My dad got a job transfer to New York after I graduated and I decided to make a new start, to try to forget you. I eventually joined the FBI and made a pretty good life for myself."

She fell silent for a while, before saying, "Listen, Zeke, it would really help if you'd take some responsibility for what happened between us. I haven't heard an apology from you yet."

"You want me to apologize?" he asked incredulously. "For something that wasn't my fault?"

The last time Zeke had apologized to a woman, he had done so under duress, pressured by his pastor to preserve harmony in the church. It had left an indelible stain on his psyche, and he steadfastly refused to go back there again. Apologies were now only given to those who deserved them, and Goldie definitely didn't fall into that category.

"You could've done more to find me," she challenged. "But you did nothing. I think you should own up to that."

He stared at her in frustration, her defensive posture reminding him of Susan, the recipient of his forced apology given the day after he'd witnessed her stealing from the collection plate one Sunday morning. When he'd raised the issue with the elders, Susan had vehemently denied the sin and claimed that Zeke had been mistaken. As it was only Zeke's word against hers, the pastor had encouraged Zeke to be the bigger person and apologize. He remembered the pastor's words distinctly: "Saying sorry is a small sacrifice in order to maintain peace with your neighbor."

Well, perhaps he didn't care whether he maintained peace with Goldie. This time, he would stick to his guns and stand firm.

"What happened was *not* my fault, so you'll be waiting a long time if you want me to take the blame." He recognized the sense of indignation in his belly—the same one he'd felt when Susan had smiled and accepted his apology, despite knowing her guilt. "You're being totally unfair."

She balked. "It's going to be mighty difficult for us to get along here if you insist on avoiding your responsibilities."

He threw his hands in the air, having heard enough. "I will not allow you to guilt trip me into taking responsibility for the past," he said. "If I do that, I'll lose respect for myself, wind up angry and isolated and have to leave the assignment."

"What? That's quite a stretch, Zeke. Are you crazy?"

"Not crazy, just eager to speak the truth."

After reluctantly apologizing to Susan, Zeke had found it impossible to enjoy the worship while watching her continue to serve, to collect the offerings and pretend as if nothing had happened. He knew that she was a thief and a liar, and yet he was the one being punished. He had eventually left his church family and joined another, a wrench that had left a mark of deep injustice etched on his heart. He had paid the price of her sin.

"We're here for a week," she said. "We'll have to find a way past this."

Sounds of movement came from the stairs, then a man called out that the forensic team had completed its analysis of the crime scene.

"How about we keep things strictly professional?" he suggested. "That's all we can do for now."

"Sure." Her tone was as snippy as scissors. "I'm fine with that."

Zeke's attention was taken by the appearance of two men in the hallway, carrying a body bag between them. He automatically lowered his head and clasped his hands at his waist. It was an involuntary reaction, one that obviously irritated Goldie, judging by the loud huff.

"What happened to your faith, Goldie?" he asked, his attitude softening. "How did you lose it?"

"That subject is off-limits," she snapped, striding from the kitchen toward Karl's voice, which was rising animatedly from somewhere on the stairs. "We're keeping things professional, remember?"

He followed her from the room, feeling the metaphorical door slam in his face. Goldie was full of anger and resentment, not only for him but for God too. And it wasn't his job to try to fix it.

On the grand carpeted stairway, Karl was agitated as he clutched his cell phone tightly to his ear.

"This is the worst possible news we could receive right now," he said into the speaker. "I agree that we need to source two more agents to replace Goldie and Zeke. I'll get on it immediately and call you back."

He ended the call, pressed one end of the

cell to his forehead and squeezed his eyes shut behind his heavy framed glasses.

"What's going on, sir?" Goldie asked, holding on to the curved banister at the bottom of the stairs. "You're not throwing Zeke and I off the case, are you? We made a promise that we wouldn't let you down."

Karl walked the remainder of the stairs with a slow and tired gait, coming to stand next to Goldie on the shiny hallway floor. Zeke didn't like the look on their boss's face, not one little bit. He moved closer, wondering what on earth had happened to see him and Goldie both ejected from the assignment within hours of arrival.

"I just spoke with Christina," Karl began. "And she told me some very disturbing news."

Christina Phillips was the special agent in charge of the FBI's Philadelphia office, a woman who Zeke heard was a no-nonsense, straight-talking leader, admired for her dedication to the job.

"What did she say?" Goldie asked.

"Leonardo and his brother are very angry about what happened here today," Karl replied. "And they want revenge for Marsha's death."

Goldie held up her hands, palms forward, fingers splayed. "Wait, are you serious? Marsha went against Leonardo's wishes by trying to harm Louisa. Why would they care that she died defying the family's orders?"

"I don't know why they care, but they do." The strain of this case was showing on Karl's lined face. "They've somehow managed to find out who fired the fatal bullet, and they've put a hit on you, Goldie. That's why you have to come off the case. You need to lay low until we figure out how to proceed. I've assigned Zeke to protect you."

Goldie's mouth dropped open as she stared at Zeke, revealing her horror and resistance to this plan of action.

"No way," she said, pacing the hall. "I refuse to let this happen. You're probably overreacting, sir. Nobody's gonna come after me."

"Oh, I think they will," Karl said strongly. "For the kind of reward that the Voltos are offering, I expect a ton of criminals to come crawling out the woodwork."

"How much are we talking about, sir?" Zeke said, his concerns rising.

Karl paused for a dramatic breath. "The Volto family has promised the sum of two million dollars to the first person who kills Goldie, and we're relying on you to help keep her alive."

TWO

Goldie replayed Karl's words in her head, convinced that she must've misheard.

"Let me get this straight," she said. "Did you just say there's a price of two million dollars on my head?"

Karl ushered both her and Zeke into the living room. "I'm sorry, Goldie, but that's exactly what I said. The Bureau is taking the threat very seriously, and we're doing all we can to ensure your safety."

"How does the Volto family have access to that kind of money?" she asked, sitting on the huge white couch next to Zeke. "I thought the FBI froze all their assets." She gestured to the opulence around her. "Apart from the ones we allowed Mrs. Volto to keep as part of her deal, of course."

"The Voltos aren't the ones supplying the cash," Karl replied. "A powerful Mafia family in Chicago has agreed to front the money on the Voltos' behalf after Leonardo begged for their help. As we already know, members of law enforcement aren't the Mafia's favorite people, unless they're on the payroll."

Goldie rested her elbows on her knees and let her forehead drop onto her cupped hands. Zeke placed a tentative palm on her back, but she stiffened and he removed it. Finding out that he had never received her letters all those years ago did nothing to ease her pain. In fact, it made it worse. Why did he not try to track her down rather than move to New York to start fresh? He could've at least *tried*. He gave up without so much as a whimper. And just like her ex-con father, Zeke was refusing to say sorry for causing so much misery.

"Who's the source of the information, sir?" Zeke asked. "Can we trust it?"

"I can't reveal too much, but an agent who's gone deep cover has gotten in touch with his handler to say that every criminal gang on the East Coast has been contacted with the hit request." He sighed. "I wish I could say that our source was unreliable, but he's not. The intel is good."

"What does this mean for me, exactly?" Goldie asked. "Do I have to go into the Witness Protection Program until this all blows over?"

"You're not a witness," Zeke said. "So you don't meet the criteria."

Karl nodded. "Technically, that's true, but the program will usually accommodate members of law enforcement who have a price on their head. Thankfully, this situation doesn't happen often, but the rules can be bent to protect our own."

"So what are we waiting for, sir?" Zeke asked. "Can we get her into a safe house right away?"

"Under normal circumstances, I'd already be organizing a safe house for her, but these are not normal circumstances. Christina has confirmed that Marsha had some inside help today."

"There's a mole?" Goldie was shocked. "In the Bureau?"

"Classified information was found in Marsha's pocket when we searched the body," Karl replied. "She had the FBI's Volto case schedule for the day, complete with the names of the agents assigned to the case, your cell numbers and what time you'd be arriving. She obviously had the old schedule because she assumed that Zeke was David McQueen when she watched Officer Diaz let him into the house. She then incapacitated Diaz, assumed his identity and waited for you to arrive."

"Could she have stolen that information from Officer Diaz himself?" Goldie asked.

"The police officers assigned to the Volto case are provided with limited details," Karl said. "The FBI is trying to maintain a very tight circle on this case." He shook his head. "Diaz doesn't have high-level clearance, so that schedule was either stolen or leaked from further up the chain. It wasn't a particularly serious breach in terms of information, but it could signal worse leaks to come."

"I should've realized something was wrong when Marsha seemed eager to come inside," Goldie chastised herself. "I can't believe she fooled me so easily."

"Don't beat yourself up about it," Zeke said. "We're all human and we all make mistakes."

Goldie avoided looking directly at him, not wanting to challenge him on his own mistakes and subsequent failure to apologize. Zeke's face had filled out over the years, his jaw now squarer and his mousy blond hair a little grayer in places, but his eyes remained unchanged, almost transparent blue. Those eyes had the power to transport her back in time, all the way back to Glenside, when she believed that her future was preordained, destined to be shared with the boy of her dreams. How fragile her dream turned out to be, and how simply it shattered. And now Zeke stubbornly and steadfastly refused to acknowledge his part in its downfall.

"We don't know where Marsha got her information," Karl said, bringing her back to the present. "It could've come from the FBI or the Philly police force, but it means that Christina wants to be supercautious about sourcing a safe house that could easily be compromised. She needs time to find the leak and shut it down."

"So I just stay here?" Goldie asked. "And make it easy for the hit men to find me?"

"Remaining in this house is the best option for now, especially considering there's a panic room for emergencies," Karl said. "It's just a temporary solution while we make a long-term plan, but we'll be leaking a fake story internally about you going into hiding in New Mexico. We're hoping to throw the bounty hunters off your scent."

Goldie's heart sank. "That means I'll have to stay inside and out of sight at all times?"

Karl nodded. "As much as possible, yes. Zeke too. I want him to shadow you."

Her heart now sank even further, right into her sneakers. "I can take care of myself, sir. I don't need a bodyguard."

"He's not a bodyguard," Karl said. "He's

your partner. Having a second pair of eyes and ears is the best way to spot any signs of danger."

"If it's all the same to you, sir, I'd rather that Zeke wasn't up in my business. That scenario's not gonna work for me."

She slid her eyes across to Zeke's and saw unbridled concern. He was deeply worried.

"This is serious," he said. "Two million dollars is a huge reward, and it'll encourage all the sleazebags and lowlifes to hunt you down. Let me help. I'll be there for you."

She snorted. "Yeah, cause you did such a good job of being there for me last time, huh?"

"You're being unreasonable," he shot back. "I was only seventeen, Goldie, just a kid. What was I supposed to do when you just vanished?"

She couldn't stop her voice from rising. "Maybe you could've intercepted the mailman and picked up my letters before your parents had a chance to destroy them?"

"I had no idea you were even writing me." He stood up. "This is ridiculous. We literally just agreed to be professional."

"This sure isn't professional behavior," Karl said, switching his gaze between them. "I didn't realize that you two had such a complicated history, but whatever's bugging you, let it go. I want to see you working together." He brought the tips of both index fingers together. "Teamwork, okay?"

Goldie was shamefaced at having lashed out. She was so full of fury and bitterness, and Zeke was bearing the brunt because she had to allocate blame somewhere. And his shoulders seemed like a good fit, especially considering that her father's shoulders had shrugged off any kind of responsibility.

"I'm sorry for my outburst, sir," she said, hanging her head. "It won't happen again."

"Good." Karl stood. "Mrs. Volto says she'll allow you to stay here for the next few days, but she wants her lawyer to negotiate a compensation package with us." He rolled his eyes. "That shady lawyer sure does love squeezing money out of the FBI."

"But Goldie's worth every penny, right, sir?" Zeke said.

"You're absolutely correct, Agent Miller," Karl replied. "We'll spare no expense to keep her out of harm's way, I can assure you of that." His cell rang in his pocket, and he headed for the kitchen. "Excuse me, guys, I need to take this."

Goldie sat silently on the sofa, wondering exactly how much money she would be costing the Bureau. Not only was Mrs. Volto demanding compensation for providing a secure hiding place, but also two new agents were being drafted onto the assignment. The cost would surely run into thousands, if not hundreds of thousands, of extra dollars. And contrary to Zeke's assessment of her value, Goldie knew she wasn't worth it. Why would she place a high value on herself when God clearly didn't?

Zeke seemed to read her thoughts. "You *are* worth it, Goldie. Whatever's going on between the two of us, you're still worth fighting for."

She shook her head. "Stop it." Kindness always brought her tears to the surface. "I know what I'm worth, and it's not this huge amount of money."

She stood up, smoothed down her T-shirt, took a deep breath and added one more brick to the wall. With her emotions running amok after Zeke's shock arrival into her life, she would have to make herself invincible.

Zeke sat next to Louisa Volto at the kitchen table while her lawyer, Willy Murphy, sat at her other side. Willy was a shrewd character, well-known in law-enforcement circles by his nickname of "The Mafia Whisperer."

He'd represented many unsavory characters within the criminal underworld, and often successfully fought off charges of murder, extortion, fraud and tax evasion. As a lawyer, he was quite brilliant. As a human being, he was sadly lacking in moral fiber.

Opposite Louisa around the oval table were Karl and Christina. The special agent in charge of the Philadelphia office didn't often make field visits, but Willy had insisted on dealing only with the top brass. Christina was clearly irritated at being dragged away from her desk and wanted to deal with the matter promptly.

"I'm sure we're all incredibly busy," she said, glancing at her watch. "So let's get straight down to business, shall we? The Bureau has agreed to a compensation package of ten thousand dollars per day to host Agent Simmons, until we find an alternative solution."

Goldie gasped, turning quickly on the balls of her feet, red curls bouncing. She was standing in the corner of the kitchen, as if trying to make herself as inconspicuous as possible. Since learning of the price on her head, she had been quiet and withdrawn.

"That's a fortune," she said, joining them at the table. "Mrs. Volto, how can you justify charging the taxpayers such a huge sum simply for letting me stay in your home?"

Louisa smoothed her expensively cut brunette bob and reached for the hand of her lawyer beneath the table, seemingly deferring the question to the expert negotiator.

"Mrs. Volto is taking an enormous risk by allowing you to remain here," Willy said sharply. "And let's not forget that she's helping the FBI to bring down one of the most powerful Mafia families in America. Once the trial is over, she'll need enough financial capital to employ bodyguards for the rest of her life. This will never be over for her."

"Or for you, Willy," Goldie suggested. "You're a Mafia traitor too, right? What's in it for you?"

"That's none of your business." He turned his head toward Christina. "Ten thousand dollars seems a little low, Agent Phillips. How about we make it twenty?"

Goldie let out a groan of irritation. "Don't let him railroad you, ma'am," she said. "You can't possibly spend that kind of money on me."

Zeke frowned. There it was again—Goldie's insinuation that her life wasn't worth a high cost. He remembered her as someone who was far more certain of her value and place in the world. What had happened to her self-esteem? It seemed to have evaporated.

Christina held out a manicured hand to Willy. "If we can agree to call it fifteen, you got yourself a deal, Mr. Murphy."

Willy leaned across the table and shook her hand. "I'll draw up a legal contract today and get it on your desk by 5:00 p.m."

Goldie sighed. "I think it's crazy."

"As I've already explained to you, Agent Simmons, witness protection is a very expensive business," Willy said. "That's why Mrs. Volto negotiated a settlement whereby she keeps this beautiful house and a sizable sum in the bank. It's her security."

"Might I remind you that the FBI offered Mrs. Volto the opportunity to enter the Witness Protection Program," Christina said. "We could've provided all the security that she and her unborn child require."

Willy let out a snorting laugh. A small man with a mop of baby curls and delicate features, his soft appearance belied his true and ruthless nature.

"Mrs. Volto doesn't want to end up living on a dusty old plain in Idaho. She's used to a high standard, and I see no reason why she should give it up."

Mrs. Volto herself now decided to speak

up. "From what I've been led to understand, Agent Phillips," she said crisply to Christina, "the reason that Agent Simmons needs to stay here is because of a mole within law enforcement. Marsha had help in gaining access to my home today, and that fault is on *you*. Why would I possibly consider entering the Witness Protection Program when you don't even trust it enough to put one of your own agents in a safe house?"

Christina swallowed and dropped her gaze to the table, apparently unable to deny these truths.

"I admit we've identified a weak link somewhere in the chain," she said diplomatically. "And we're working very hard to track down the source, but I can assure you that the Witness Protection Program has a strong record of success." She smiled curtly. "And we don't resettle clients on dusty plains in Idaho unless they really love potatoes."

"Well, I want to stay right here in Gladwyne," Mrs. Volto said. "And I would appreciate receiving payments on a daily basis for Goldie's room and board. I expect the first one by midnight tonight."

Christina nodded. "I'll personally see to it."

"Let's go, Willy." Mrs. Volto stood, still holding her lawyer's hand. "I have some per-

sonal matters to discuss with you in the conservatory."

Christina began to gather her paperwork.
"I should be leaving too. There's a ton of stuff
to do at the office." She smiled at Goldie.
"I'm working on your situation, Agent Simmons. The Witness Protection Program has
approved our request, so as soon as it's safe,
we'll get you moved."

"But witness protection is only temporary,
right?" Goldie asked. "Just until this all blows
over?"

"Let's take it one day at a time," Christina
replied. "And see how things develop."

"I can't believe I'm costing the Bureau fifteen grand for every day I stay here," Goldie
said sadly. "And that's only a fraction of the
total cost, I'm sure."

"Don't worry about it." Christina tapped
across the tiled floor in her patent heels, accompanied by Karl. "Not only is it vital that
we keep you safe, it's important that we keep
Mrs. Volto happy. She takes the stand in two
days' time, and she's seven months pregnant.
The money isn't important."

"It's true," Zeke said, sliding across to take
the seat next to her. "Why do you place such
a low value on yourself? Your life is precious,
Goldie, and don't forget it."

She stared at her hands, fingers intertwined on the table. "I used to think that way too, but I don't know what changed. I just don't see myself as important anymore."

"Why?"

She took a deep breath. "I guess I figured that if God Himself didn't listen to my prayers, then why should anybody else care about me? I tried to hold on to my faith for a long time, Zeke, I really did, but I could feel it slipping away every day." She shrugged. "And now it's gone."

"I wish I could help." He took a risk by placing a hand on her shoulder. "That's gotta be rough."

She let out a strangled laugh. "Ironically, my lack of faith helped a lot when I was in the army because I turned really reckless and gung ho. I became known as fearless, but it was because I didn't care about my safety. In the end, I knew I had to leave the military because I'd end up getting myself killed. And since joining the FBI I managed to build up some self-esteem. I was doing really well until…"

He finished her sentence. "Until I showed up."

"Yeah. You remind me of the dark times I went through. I feel bad about myself again, like I'm not worthy of affection or attention or fifteen thousand dollars a day."

"You know that I would spend every cent I own on your well-being, right?"

She shook her head almost imperceptibly. "I can't forgive you, Zeke."

He clenched his jaw. There was nothing he needed to be forgiven for, because he had done nothing wrong.

"Can't you just pretend to be sorry?" she asked. "For my sake? Throughout my whole life, nobody's ever given me an apology for what I've been through."

"Not even your father?"

She snorted a laugh. "Especially not my father. He was released from prison eight years ago and I gave him one last chance to say sorry for his mistakes. Do you know what he said?"

"What?"

"He said he only embezzled the money to give me and my sister a good life. He said I was ungrateful for his sacrifice."

Zeke was silent for a moment. "He's a real jerk."

"Yeah. That's why I cut him out of my life."

Zeke could see why his apology mattered so much to Goldie. It was about giving her closure on the past, an acknowledgment that she was wronged and treated badly. But it was unfair to focus that negative energy on him.

"I'm not your father, Goldie," he said. "I'm a good man."

"Then why can't you apologize for hurting me?"

"It would be a hollow apology," he said. "I've given a hollow apology once before and it didn't help anybody, least of all the person who received it."

As far as he was concerned, Susan had gone unpunished, free of the consequences of her wrongdoing and free to remain an active and respected member of the church. But her sin would surely be eating away at her. He often wondered if he should've refused the pastor's request and dug in his heels instead. But he had chosen the easy path, one that maintained a peaceful congregation.

He would not sacrifice his principles for the sake of harmony again. He was hurt and mad just like Goldie, mostly by her ridiculous assertion that he could've done more to track her down after she vanished. Zeke was just a teenager at the time, in the days before social media, with no idea where to start in tracing a missing person. He deserved sympathy too.

If Goldie thought he was going to take the blame for the tragedies of the past, she was sorely mistaken. This time he would plant his feet firmly on the side of truth.

Goldie stared at the enormous TV screen fixed to the wall in the living room, transfixed by the news report. A reporter was standing at the end of the street, Mrs. Volto's house visible in the background, police tape closing off the road to vehicles. A heavy police presence was still in the area.

"The wife of alleged mobster Joseph Volto was gunned down by an FBI agent inside this home earlier today," the reporter said into her microphone.

"You did not gun her down," Zeke muttered as he sat beside Goldie. "She was given plenty of opportunity to give herself up."

The reporter continued speaking as the camera homed in on Mrs. Volto's estate. "Twenty-nine-year-old Marsha Volto was shot and killed by an agent assigned to protect Louisa Volto, wife of alleged mafia boss Leonardo Volto, as she prepares to testify against her husband and his brother this Thursday. And it would seem that the agent who killed Marsha Volto is now in the line of fire herself. There are multiple reports of a bounty having been placed on the head of Agent Marigold Simmons by the Volto family, who have promised the sum of two million dollars to the first person to hunt her down."

Zeke groaned. "This is terrible reporting. They're basically advertising the hit on behalf of the Mafia."

"Agent Simmons is no longer in the residence of Mrs. Volto, and her whereabouts are unknown," the reporter continued. "While the FBI remains tight-lipped about the shooting incident, the Bureau has confirmed that Agent Simmons has gone into hiding far away from Pennsylvania." A slight smile touched her lips. "And with a bounty of two million dollars on her head, who could blame her?"

Zeke picked up the remote control from the armrest and turned off the television.

"We should complain to the news station," he said. "That was totally unethical."

"It won't make a difference," Goldie replied. "Leave it alone, Zeke."

"That sounds defeatist to me. I'll ask Karl to make a complaint on your behalf."

Goldie slumped forward, her hair falling over her face. She felt so empty and alone in this situation, having been stripped of power and authority. She could no longer make her own decisions and was entirely reliant on others, Zeke in particular as he had been assigned to shadow her.

"I learned a long time ago that the only person I can rely on is myself," she said. "But now I have no control over my life. I'm stuck in this gilded cage while other people get to make all my choices and take care of me. It's like being a child again."

"Try to think of it as a blessing," he said. "Perhaps the time is right for you to slow down and make some changes in your life."

She couldn't help but laugh. "Think of it as a blessing? That's a good one."

She had irritated him. The flare of his nostrils told her so.

"Not everything in your life can be controlled," he said. "When something bad happens, you have two choices—you can get mad about it or you can try to change it, however limited you are."

"I choose the mad option."

He clicked his tongue. "That figures."

Now she was irritated too. "It's all been so easy for you, hasn't it, Zeke? You grew up in a nice big house with two great parents and a hot meal every evening. You never had to worry about your father gambling away the grocery money, and you didn't have to hide behind the couch when debt collectors knocked on the door. You never had to watch your dad stand up in church and proclaim God's goodness right after telling you to keep your mouth shut about the eviction notice you got the previous day." Her heart was hammering. "It's easy to see hardship as a blessing when you've known nothing but privilege."

"I lived all those hardships with you, Goldie. I was the only person you confided in and I carried the burden with you. Or at least I tried to."

Zeke was right. He *had* helped to carry the burden, and that was why she'd struggled so very much after moving to Ohio. With nobody to lean on, she had turned to God, pouring out her misery to Him. Yet, just like Zeke, He apparently did nothing.

"I know that my life has been more privileged than yours," he continued. "But I can't do anything about that. All I can do is try to understand your journey and work out ways I can help you heal. Two things I can definitely do are pray for you and protect you."

She raised her eyes to the ceiling. Zeke's words sounded so incredibly naive.

"When my dad dragged us all to Cleveland and rented a rat-infested apartment in a sleazy neighborhood, I realized something." She turned her head dead center to his. "I realized that I can't trust God to care for me." Her voice dropped to barely a whisper. "And I can't trust you either. Save your prayers, Zeke, because they don't work."

He took a long time to consider his response, rubbing his chin.

"Once again, I don't think you're being very fair to me," he said. "Or to God for that matter. Your childhood was awful, something no kid should ever have to suffer, but look at you now. You've served your country, and you're a highly respected FBI agent. Your life turned out pretty good in the end, so why are you still so mad about the past?"

She didn't want to answer. Zeke's probing questions were forcing her to confront issues that she would rather keep buried deep.

"My life turned out okay, but it's too late for me to have the things I truly wanted," she said. "I'm nearly forty years old and I'm still alone." She crossed her arms. "I wanted to get married and have kids and give them the beautiful family life I never had. That's what we were meant to have together, Zeke. It's what I thought God had planned out for me." She threw back her head and laughed. "I'm such an idiot."

He ran a hand down his face. "Oh boy,

Goldie. There's a whole lot going on in your head."

"I believe the official term for someone like me is a hot mess," she said. "And it's not a great place to be when there's a price on your head."

"I told you that I'd keep you safe," he said. "Whatever happens, I'm here for you."

"Yeah. You said that over twenty years ago, so you can see why I might be a little skeptical."

Now his patience seemed to snap. "Let it go, Marigold. What's done is done and you have to move past it. Your life is in danger, so let's focus on that instead, okay?"

"I already told you, Zeke, it's Goldie now." She picked up the remote control and flicked on the TV. "Marigold died a long time ago."

Karl looked to be tense and stressed as he entered the house followed by a brown-haired man and a blonde woman. It was pitch-dark outside, night having fallen on a long and eventful day.

Closing and locking the door behind him, Karl motioned for the two strangers to sit in the living room. Zeke waited for Goldie to turn off the TV, but, when she failed to do so, he reached for the remote instead. Goldie seemed to be in a world of her own, and he tried not to judge her too harshly for zoning out. She had a lot on her mind. Yet it did not excuse her rudeness.

"Zeke, Goldie," Karl began. "This is Special Agent Angela Martin and Special Agent Garth Cooper. They're here to replace you on the protection detail for Mrs. Volto. Agent Cooper has been drafted onto the case because he's an expert criminal investigator."

"An expert investigator?" Zeke queried, shaking hands with his new colleagues. "You really went all out, huh, sir?"

"Garth has a great track record, and I wanted to get him onto the assignment to utilize his skills and experience." Karl took off his jacket and rolled up his sleeves. "He's got a ton of contacts in the criminal underworld, so if Goldie's position here is leaked, he should be the first to know." He looked over at Garth. "Isn't that right, Agent Cooper?"

"Absolutely." Garth sat next to Goldie and leaned in close. "I've been briefed on your situation, and I want you to know that I'll do whatever I can to make sure your whereabouts remain a closely guarded secret. I'm sorry you've been targeted just for doing your job, Agent Simmons, but that's the risk we take in law enforcement, right?"

"Please," she replied. "Call me Goldie."

As Zeke watched their introduction unfold, he found an unpleasant and unwanted sensation sneak into his veins. After twenty-one years of being apart, could he still be attracted to Goldie? Was he feeling a stab of jealousy at seeing her sitting so close to another man? He and Goldie had been besotted with each other as teenagers, spending every possible moment together. He would've expected his attraction to have waned after all this time, yet she still made his heart skip. Considering her strong hostility toward him, he consoled himself with the likelihood that any lingering feelings would be burned to ashes before long.

"Garth and Angela have been brought in from our headquarters in Washington," Karl said. "I thought it would be best to recruit outside the state, given that we still don't know who passed the classified document on to Marsha."

"Do we have any leads on that?" Zeke asked.

"None at all, I'm afraid," Karl replied with a sorrowful shake of the head. "Everybody with access to the Volto case file seems to

check out. But we're leaving no stone un-
turned in the investigation."

Angela wandered through the room, running her hand across the marble mantel and
sculptures. "This is the most beautiful home
I've ever seen," she said. "It's a shame it's
been built with drugs, racketeering and extortion."

"While I agree with you, Agent Martin,"
Karl said, "I'd rather you kept those kinds
of opinions to yourself when meeting Mrs.
Volto. We don't want to upset her after her
recent ordeal. She says the baby is doing fine,
but she won't see a doctor. She's incredibly
jittery about strangers coming into her home,
so cut her a lot of slack, okay?"

"Sure thing." Angela pointed to the hallway. "Shall Garth and I go meet her now?"

Karl led the way. "I'll introduce you. She's
in the conservatory with her lawyer, and you
have my permission to cut him no slack at
all." He turned his head as he left the room,
pointing to the window. "Close those drapes.
All points of entry must be covered from now
on."

Zeke went to the window and dragged one
of the heavy drapes across it, before noticing
Goldie with her head in her hands yet again,
her body language radiating misery.

"My life is over," she said quietly. "I only just fully realized it. The Mafia hit on me won't ever expire. It'll just run and run until I'm found. And then someone will pocket two million dollars and I'll be dead."

He wasn't sure what to say. It was true that most people caught in the crosshairs of the Mafia disappeared, either into the Witness Protection Program or a shallow grave.

"The Witness Protection Program can help you," he said, going to sit next to her. "They'll relocate you, give you a new life. You'll be safe."

She ran her fingers through her beautiful, long curls, pulling back the strands to reveal her porcelain, freckled skin and vivid green eyes. To his surprise she suddenly smiled, her childlike dimples taking years off her true age.

"I guess that's the one good thing about having to start over again," she said. "I can change my awful name. I've always hated it."

"Stop it," he said, punching her playfully. "Marigold is cute, kind of like sunshine."

"You only think it's cute because your name is worse," she said.

"What?" He was glad that the mood was lightening. "What's wrong with Zeke?"

"It sounds like a birdcall. Or a zipper."

They both began to laugh, naturally slipping back into their old familiarity, Goldie leaning against Zeke with her shoulder and he resting his cheek on top of her head. For a few seconds, the years fell away and they were teenagers again, hanging out, being happy. Without thinking, Zeke reached out and held her hand. It was something he'd done a million times over.

"What are you doing?" Goldie jumped up. "Everything is different now."

He was mortified at his lapse. "I'm sorry." Just like Goldie, he didn't want to stir the pot. "I guess the old habits are still strong."

She stood, bathed in the light of the overhead bulb, her hair shining like copper wire, lustrous and glossy. But something else was glinting on her head, something red and skittish—a dot that bounced across her hair and came to rest on her forehead.

"Goldie!" he yelled, springing from the couch. "Get down."

He had just enough time to wrestle her to the carpet before a bullet shattered the window and lodged in the wall above their heads.

THREE

In the silence that followed the bullet, Goldie and Zeke remained on the floor, like spoons in a drawer, Zeke behind Goldie and clutching her tight. He heard footsteps and raised voices heading their way from the conservatory, obviously drawn by the gunshot.

"What's going on?"

Karl entered the room only to be immediately sent back by another bullet, this one ricocheting off the mantel and slamming hard onto the heavy glass coffee table. The surface shattered like a car windshield, creating a perfect hole surrounded by a hundred fanning cracks.

"Stay back!" Goldie yelled. "There's a shooter out there."

"I'll get Louisa and Willy into the panic room," Karl shouted. "And I'll call for a SWAT team." He peeked around the door, moving his head just in time to avoid a bullet splitting the wooden door frame above his head. "You two stay where you are." Zeke detected anger in his boss's voice. "I thought I told you to pull the drapes."

Zeke knew that the fault lay with him. He had allowed Goldie's despondency to distract him from the task. But laying blame didn't much matter now, because somewhere outside was a sniper with a line of sight between their hiding position and the door. They were trapped.

A series of shots tore through the closed drape, causing random damage, hoping to seek out their prey. A vase of lilies on a plinth burst with an explosion of water and glass and petals, and Zeke scooted across the carpet, dragging Goldie with him, positioning them both at the base of the sofa, where they had some degree of protection. Bullets peppered the silk cushions, sending tiny white feathers dancing through the air. The shooter was doing his best to flush them out into the open, into the space not obscured by the drape.

"Don't move," Zeke said into Goldie's ear, cradling her head, feeling her curls twine through his fingers. "He wants us to run."

As if to prove his theory was right, an even more ferocious hailstorm came raining down, bullets fired in quick succession spraying the wall, creating small craters in the plaster, smashing pictures in their frames, shearing limbs off the upright statues and sending the television set crashing to the floor.

When the noise abated, Zeke heard only the sound of Goldie's breathing, heavy and quick. She had curled tightly against him and feathers had settled on her hair, as soft and gentle as fresh snow. Directly above her head was a ragged hole in the corner of the couch, the exit site of a bullet. Having entered through the back, it had bypassed the frame and traveled all the way to the front, and was now firmly lodged in the wooden leg of the shattered coffee table. It was the sight of this bullet, so close to Goldie's head, that persuaded Zeke to change his mind about running.

"Listen to me, Goldie," he said, taking advantage of the lull in gunfire. "I'll provide cover while you get out of here. Start your run on the count of three."

"No," she protested. "I won't leave you here all alone."

"Please," he begged. "You said that you can't forgive me for not trying to find you all those years ago." This was one sacrifice he was prepared to make in order to save her life. "Well, let me try to make up for it now."

"That's not fair on you," she said. "How about I provide cover while you escape?"

"The longer we spend arguing about a plan, the less time we'll have to actually carry it out." He wriggled away slightly and took his gun from its holster. "You ready? Go on my signal, okay?"

But they'd run out of time, because a new hailstorm of bullets began to rain down, creating another cacophony of noise. The huge gilded mirror above the mantel broke into several pieces, and razor-sharp shards started to topple from the frame in their direction. They now had no choice but to move in order to escape the makeshift knives. Zeke pushed Goldie from the path of the shards and she rolled over and over on the carpet, across the debris and strewn feathers. She came to rest beneath a wide dresser, almost certainly an antique, and lay there, facedown, hands covering her ears.

Meanwhile, Zeke crawled on his forearms like a soldier in battle around the sofa and to the window, where he sat in a hunch, knees drawn up to his chest. All he could think of was how to force the shooter to stop and protect Goldie's life. With the sound of sirens floating on the wind, he sprang up and stood at the broken window, firing his gun into the air, high enough to be sure of hitting nothing. Firing blind, he just wanted to spook the shooter, to make him believe that a counterattack was taking place. The strategy worked. The incoming gunfire ceased immediately, and Zeke was able to confidently shout an order to run.

Goldie scrambled out from beneath the dresser, and Zeke ran to her, grabbed her hand and pulled her from the room. Only when they reached the safety of the hallway, far away from any windows, did he allow himself to feel a flood of relief. And with Karl anxiously standing guard at the front door, Zeke pulled Goldie into his arms and buried his face in her hair, thanking God for bringing them out alive.

Goldie paced in her bedroom with the windows locked and blinds drawn. She felt like an animal in a cage, forced to continually walk around the small space for exercise and to release her pent-up anxiety. She'd been confined to her room for the entire day, as workers and tradesmen came and went, cleaning up the destruction of yesterday's incident. Of all the things Goldie hated most, solitude took the number one spot. She preferred to stay busy, to fill her time with activity and chase away the painful thoughts that often crept into her mind.

A soft knock sounded on the door. "Hey, it's me. Can I come in?"

"Sure."

At that point, she welcomed any company, even Zeke's.

He slipped into the room and closed the door behind him. He was carrying a mug of coffee, black and hot and just what she needed at that moment. Handing it to her, he smiled, and she turned away, not wanting to see the tiny little chip on his front tooth. She'd been with him when it had happened, fooling around by the lake, using a homemade rope swing to splash into the water. Zeke had miscalculated his trajectory and hit a shallower part than he'd intended, cutting his lip on the stony bottom. The chip in the enamel of his front tooth was minuscule, barely noticeable to anyone but her, but she found herself looking for it whenever he smiled, reminding her of the carefree kids they used to be.

"You all right?" he asked. "Must be tough being shut away up here for so long, huh?"

She sat on the chair in the corner of the large room, which was tastefully furnished with French-style wardrobes and dressers, all powder blue with gold handles.

"I guess I'll have to get used to it," she said. "Who knew that being in hiding would actually involve some real hiding?"

He smiled again, sat on her bed and leaned forward to rest his forearms on his knees. He was barefoot, wearing jeans and a checkered shirt, its pinky hue suiting his olive tones. She marveled at how much he had filled out over the years, no longer skinny and adolescent but strong and muscled. He was more handsome than ever, and she wondered why he hadn't been snapped up for marriage by now.

"The trade workers are almost done downstairs," he said. "The new window has been fitted and a brand-new sofa just arrived in a truck, so you'll be able to stop hiding out up here pretty soon."

"I guess Karl wants to have a meeting for the incident report," she said, sipping her coffee. "Mrs. Volto will need stronger security measures in place when she travels to the courthouse. The ferocity of this attack changes everything, and it's made worse by the fact the shooter managed to escape."

Zeke narrowed his blue eyes, wrinkling his brow. "Do you think last night's shooter was targeting Mrs. Volto?"

"Of course. Don't you?"

"No, I don't. I think he was a bounty hunter and he was targeting you."

She tucked her feet beneath her on the plush chenille chair. "That's highly unlikely, Zeke. We knew that Mrs. Volto's life would be in danger when she turned on her husband, and that theory was proven correct by the attack she faced from her sister-in-law yesterday. The shooter was probably Marsha's accomplice, trying to finish the job that she failed to do."

He shook his head. "I don't think the two attacks are linked. Marsha came here for Mrs. Volto, but the shooter came here for *you*."

"Why would you think that?"

"Because the laser sight of the gun was seeking you out." He stood, padded across the carpet and placed the tip of his index finger gently on her forehead. "The red dot was right here."

Goldie didn't remember seeing the laser sight of a rifle, nor even realize that danger was stalking them. Zeke's prompt action had saved her life, and she would be forever grateful to him. That was at least one positive emotion she could associate with him.

"Karl told me that the investigators found a lot of shell casings on the roof terrace of the house across the street, so we know the shooter was there," Goldie said. "There isn't a great line of sight from that angle, and these old windows have the original glass that can distort the view a little. The shooter saw a woman, assumed it was Mrs. Volto and took his shots."

"I'm not buying it, Goldie. You're tall and slim, with this huge mane of red hair, and Mrs. Volto is much shorter with dark hair, not to mention the fact that she's seven months pregnant."

Goldie conceded that Zeke might have a point. "What does Karl say?"

"Karl thinks the same as you. He says the shooter was Marsha's accomplice, trying to take out Mrs. Volto before she testifies at trial. He says it's the most likely explanation, given the circumstances."

"The circumstances?"

"Agent Cooper reported that his underworld contacts have all taken the bait put out by the FBI. A false story was leaked by the Bureau, which puts you in New Mexico, so that's where the hunters are focused."

"Okay." She shrugged. "Well, that settles it." She stood and walked to the window, pulling the blind just an inch aside and peering out. "Why do I have to stay in this jail cell if all the bad guys think I'm in New Mexico?"

Zeke rushed to her side and pushed the blind back into place. "Stop it, Goldie. That shooter will come back for you, and if you don't take extreme precautions, he'll succeed next time. Why do I get the feeling you're not taking this threat seriously?"

She rounded on him, coffee sloshing onto her fingers. "What do you want me to do, Zeke?" She could feel herself slipping into her old, reckless army ways, not caring about her safety at all. "You want me to live in a container with some air holes cut out? Or maybe I could take up residence in the panic room. I hear it's pretty nice for a metal box."

He sighed. "I just want you to be safe. I lost you once, and I don't want to lose you again."

"You didn't lose me, Zeke," she said hotly. "You let me go. There's a difference."

"Not this again." His temper was clearly fraying. "I didn't know where to start in trying to find you. Nobody knew anything, and I asked literally everyone in town." He ran his fingers through his hair repeatedly. "My failure to trace you had a huge effect on me, and I joined the FBI in the first place just to learn how to track people down."

"So why didn't you try to find me later on?" she asked. "If the Bureau taught you how to trace people why didn't you trace me?"

"I don't know. I thought you didn't want me to find you. I figured you'd have come back to Glenside if you'd wanted to be with me."

"I *did* come back to Glenside." She was fighting the tears. "And you'd moved away without even leaving a forwarding address."

"You didn't come back for eighteen months, Goldie," he said with exasperation. "Why did you wait so long?"

"Do you have any idea how much a bus ticket from Cleveland to Philadelphia costs? It took me forever to save up that money." She wiped away a tear. "I was devastated to find out you'd gone. It was like a stab to the heart."

He turned in circles, apparently groping for the right words to say. "Well, you could've tried a little harder yourself," he said defensively. "You could've spoken to my neighbors or the folks at church. Somebody would've had a forwarding address for me."

"I thought you didn't want to see me." She dropped her gaze to the floor. "After you didn't answer any of my letters, why would I run around trying to find your new address? I assumed you'd moved away because you'd rejected me."

"And I assumed *you* rejected *me*."

"Well, it's not my fault."

He crossed his arms. "And it's not mine either."

"Thanks for the coffee," she said irritably. "That's all I need from you right now."

He stood in silence for a few seconds, shaking his head. "Will we ever find a way past this?"

She tilted her head to the side. "Perhaps you could find your way to the door first."

He gave a tense smile, turned and started walking. "This is stupid, you know that, right?"

Of course she knew it was stupid, but she was mad. Mad at Zeke, mad at herself, mad at God and mad at the world.

And somebody had to take the blame for her unhappiness.

The conservatory was dark, with heavy blinds covering each window. Christina had ordered a complete blackout, demanding that every blind be lowered and every drape closed, both day and night. It had given the house a morbid atmosphere, and Zeke was reminded of horror movies, where knife wielding bad guys jumped out of dark corners without warning.

Christina had called each occupant of the house into the conservatory for what she called a "crisis meeting," and she now walked around the air-conditioned room, switching on lamps and inviting people to sit on the wicker chairs.

"I'm sorry that we've had to cover the windows on such a beautifully sunny evening," she said, taking a seat next to Karl. "But we suffered two attacks yesterday, so we're not taking any chances."

"My client's living room was utterly destroyed by the gunman," Willy said, seated next to Mrs. Volto on a small sofa, their knees touching. "Will she be compensated for all the damaged artwork?"

Zeke and Goldie exchanged a glance of exasperation. This was one thing they could agree on—Willy really was a shyster. And Zeke certainly knew that he and Goldie needed to find some common ground, because they'd been skittering around each other like cats on a roof since their earlier argument. Yet Zeke's commitment to the truth didn't waver. He would not apologize.

"I would imagine that Mrs. Volto is insured?" Christina smiled tensely, pen hovering above a clipboard. "She could file a claim."

"Why should Mrs. Volto file a claim on her insurance when it was the FBI's fault?"

Willy slid his beady eyes over to Goldie. "The gunman was targeting your agent. Therefore, you are liable for any damage she is responsible for."

"Hang on a minute," Zeke said, coming to her defense. "Goldie didn't shoot up the room. It's not fair to blame her."

"Isn't it?" Willy looked at Zeke atop the glasses he sometimes wore, which Zeke suspected were fake lenses, intended to make him appear more intelligent. "Agent Simmons has a bounty on her head and the gunman was hoping to claim the prize. She's a liability here, so I'd like my client not only to be compensated for her damaged artwork and antiques but to receive a higher daily rate for hosting Agent Simmons."

"No!" Karl was obviously annoyed. "Goldie's presence here is a well-guarded secret, whereas your client doesn't try to hide her whereabouts. The attacker obviously came here to eliminate Mrs. Volto, and he mistook our agent for your client."

Mrs. Volto threw back her head and laughed. "That's nonsense. I already made it clear to the FBI that my husband would never order my death while I'm carrying his child. I'm not in any danger here."

Christina fixed her with a steely stare.

"Then what was Marsha doing holding a vase over your head yesterday?"

Mrs. Volto flushed. "That was different. Marsha and I argued and that's why she attacked me. She wasn't going to kill me."

"You still haven't given us a full statement regarding the conversation that took place between you and Marsha." Christina didn't let her gaze waver. "What exactly did you argue about?"

"Marsha came to check on me and the baby on behalf of my husband," Mrs. Volto said. "She said I wasn't providing Leonardo with enough updates on the pregnancy. She then said I would make a terrible mother and we argued." She pursed her red lips. "That's all there was to it."

Zeke and Goldie exchanged another glance, clearly sharing the same concern. Mrs. Volto was hiding something.

"My client really wasn't expecting Agent Simmons's presence to cause so much carnage," Willy said. "So I think that a daily rate of twenty-five thousand dollars is more appropriate, considering the high element of danger involved."

"I already explained that the Bureau doesn't believe Goldie was the target here," Christina said.

"I beg to differ." If snakes could smile, Willy nailed it. "Twenty-five thousand dollars a day seems only fair for your agent to continue residing here."

"This is wrong," Zeke said, interrupting the negotiations. "It doesn't really matter who was the intended target of the bullets. Mr. Murphy, is it really worth haggling over the safeguarding of someone's life?"

"My client needs the extra income," Willy replied curtly. "Money will set her free."

Zeke clicked his tongue in annoyance. "I think it's the truth that sets us free," he said. "Money enslaves us."

"The truth is all well and good, Agent Miller, but it doesn't pay the bills, does it?" Willy turned his attention back to Christina. "Shall we say one hundred thousand for the damaged artwork and twenty-five thousand a day for hosting Agent Simmons?"

Goldie opened her mouth to protest, but Christina held up a hand to silence her. "I'll agree to the terms, Mr. Murphy, but I once again strongly refute the suggestion that yesterday's gun attack was directed at Goldie. Your client is in serious danger, and you both seem to be in total denial about it."

Until this moment, the new additions to the FBI team, Garth and Angela, had been sitting quietly, simply observing the conversation, but now Garth decided to speak up.

"I agree with SAC Phillips, Mr. Murphy," he said. "I have extensive contacts in the criminal underworld, and I can assure you that Goldie's whereabouts are unknown in those kinds of circles. Your client's pregnancy didn't protect her from two attacks yesterday, and your complacency could get her killed."

"I won't get killed." Mrs. Volto stood up abruptly. "Do I really have to be here? I'm tired and I'd like an early night. I have to testify in court the day after tomorrow so I need to rest."

Christina regarded Mrs. Volto for a few moments, her eyes coming to rest on her large stomach. The FBI agent's attitude then appeared to soften and she smiled, possibly considering why it was important to reduce Mrs. Volto's stress levels. "Of course," she said. "Get some sleep and try not to worry. We've increased the security outside your home, and even Officer Diaz has insisted on returning to guard duty. He's determined to make up for his mistake yesterday, so you can rest easy. How is the baby doing?"

Mrs. Volto placed a hand on her belly. "He or she is playing football in there."

"That's good," Christina said with a more

sincere smile. "Our priority is always to keep you and your baby safe, Mrs. Volto."

"And Goldie," Zeke interjected. "We're safeguarding three lives here, right?"

"Absolutely," Christina said. "That's why you're here, Zeke—to be Goldie's guardian. We all have to work together to make sure we keep our eyes and ears open at all times."

"Will you walk me upstairs, Willy?" Mrs. Volto asked, holding out a hand. "I have a touch of sciatica today."

Her lawyer jumped up. "Of course." He linked an arm through hers. "I'll come back downstairs to discuss paperwork with Agent Phillips once you're tucked in bed."

The six FBI agents in the room all stood while Mrs. Volto made her way to the stairs, assisted by Willy. Then they sat, silent for a while, until Goldie finally said her first words since entering the conservatory.

"I should leave."

Zeke had been expecting this kind of protest from her. "Don't be hasty, Goldie," he said. "This is the safest place for you to be right now."

"He's right," Angela agreed. "We've got your back, Agent Simmons."

"But what if Willy's right?" she said. "What if the shooter really did come here to kill me? That means I'm placing everyone in danger." She twined her fingers together. "I *am* a liability."

Zeke decided to say nothing more about his theory that Goldie was the true target of the sniper's bullets. It didn't jibe with the opinions of the rest of the team, and he'd be shot down in flames instantly. Besides, he wanted to keep Goldie where he could look after her, and avoid her being moved to another safe house, far away from his protection. No matter how much she infuriated him, he still wanted to be close to her.

"Listen to me, Goldie," Garth said. "Nobody outside of this house knows you're here. You have to trust me on that."

"Are you sure?"

"Absolutely."

"Zeke's not so sure," she said. "He agrees with Willy." She turned her head toward him. "Isn't that right?"

"It doesn't matter what I think," he replied quickly. "I probably got it wrong."

"I thought you never got things wrong."

"When I'm wrong, I'll admit it," he said, knowing that they both understood he was no longer referring to the case. "But I won't be pushed into admitting a mistake when I didn't make one."

Predictably, a tense atmosphere settled between them, which was deftly spotted and diffused by Karl.

"Zeke concurs that the shooter was targeting Mrs. Volto," he said. "That puts everyone in agreement. We'll need to be hypervigilant to any potential threats, not only to Mrs. Volto but to Goldie also. We're on a double protection assignment here." He looked across at Goldie. "I assume you'll reconsider your plans to leave. You have the support of a great team here, and Zeke is a very capable protector."

She stared at her hands. "I don't want to be a nuisance," she said. "I especially don't want anyone to take a risk for me."

Christina knitted her eyebrows. "You're worth our time and effort, Agent Simmons. You're one of us. Can I have your assurance that you won't make plans to leave this house without my approval?"

As Zeke waited for an answer, Goldie suddenly locked eyes with him, and he saw more than he bargained for. He saw anger, bitterness, worry and the denial of her worth. But more than that, he saw the well of pain inside, the rejection she'd been carrying for twenty-one long years. Her eyes seemed to be imploring him to turn back the clock and make things right again, to heal her wounded heart. The problem was that he couldn't make anything right. What they'd once had was beautiful and innocent and fragile, and it had been broken beyond repair. A false apology wouldn't change a thing. He knew that from experience.

"I'll stay," she said. "But if it looks like I'm compromising the safety of Mrs. Volto and all of you guys, I'm outta here. I'm tough. I can survive on my own out there."

Zeke immediately saw through the act she'd built up to protect herself against the world. She wasn't tough. She was scared and lonely and in need of comfort.

Yet he wasn't able to provide it. All he could do was keep her safe and pray that she would eventually find her way out of the darkness.

Goldie brushed her hair at the dressing table in her bedroom, making long smooth strokes, the way her mother had taught her when she was a child.

"Your hair is a crown," her mom used to say. "And yours is special because it's like an orange sunset."

She put down the brush and stared at her reflection, amazed at how much she now resembled her mother, a woman who died from a heart defect at the age of fifty-five while Goldie's father was incarcerated. By that time, Goldie was surrounded by a new family in the army, and she relied heavily on her colleagues to see her through the loss, but it had been a bitter blow. Her mother had done her best as a parent, tried to protect Goldie and her sister from the worst of her father's tantrums, and Goldie was thankful to her for that. In an ideal world, her mom would've left her husband long before he ruined all their lives, but that was water under the bridge now. What was done was done.

With her mom passed on, her sister moved overseas and her ex-con father wholeheartedly kicked out of her life, Goldie was entirely alone. And boy did she feel the loneliness right at that moment. With nothing but this house to fill her days, she was struggling to hold back thoughts of lost chances and failed opportunities. Instead of growing the family she'd always wanted, she'd spent too many years eating meals for one and attending everyone's wedding but her own. Being around Zeke made the struggle ten times worse. He was nothing more than a painful reminder of what might've been and, what was more, he expressed no remorse for breaking her heart.

After losing him, she'd given up on love, and now deeply regretted not trying harder to find someone else.

After taking off her robe and straightening her nightgown, she pulled back the covers on her bed, ready to turn in for the night. But a noise caught her attention. Was there a fly in her room? Slowly padding around the bed, she strained to listen to the buzzing sound, which was rising in intensity with each second.

"What *is* that?" she said to herself, sliding her arms back into her robe and securing the belt. "It's like a million mosquitoes."

Soon enough, she heard doors opening onto the landing, feet on the stairs, voices mingling with the buzz. She slipped her gun into the pocket of her robe and opened her own door, stepping out straight into the path of Zeke, who was wearing sweatpants and an inside-out T-shirt. He'd clearly gotten dressed in a rush.

"What's that noise?" she asked.

"We're gonna find out." He glanced down the hallway at Mrs. Volto's closed bedroom door. "You need to stay upstairs with Mrs. Volto. Angela's on night duty so she'll be downstairs keeping watch."

Then he was gone, flitting down the

stairs in his sneakers, stopping at the bottom to flash her a wide smile. She hated herself for allowing her stomach to flutter. He shouldn't have that kind of power any longer. She thought she was over him. Much to her irritation, she was wrong.

Shaking her head free of thoughts of Zeke, she walked to Mrs. Volto's room and knocked on the door.

"Mrs. Volto," she called. "There's a noise outside that's being investigated right now, so don't worry. Everything is under control."

Muffled voices came from inside, one clearly male, sounding panicked and possibly hostile. Without hesitation, Goldie pulled her gun from her pocket and flung the door wide, holding her weapon aloft.

"Stop right there," she said, taking aim in the darkness. "Who's here? Put your hands in the air."

As her eyes adjusted to the gloom, she made out the shape of a man by the bed, wearing tailored pants and roughly pulling on a shirt over a rumpled undershirt. She recognized the mop of baby curls immediately.

"Mr. Murphy?" she asked. "Is that you?"

"Yes, yes, it's me," Willy said in annoyance, buttoning the shirt. "How dare you barge in here."

"I heard a man's voice." She lowered her weapon. "I'm sorry. I had no idea you two were…" She stopped. "I thought there was an intruder."

Mrs. Volto was in bed, her knees drawn up and the duvet gripped tightly beneath her chin. Only her pale and anxious face was visible.

"Please," she said imploringly. "Don't say anything to anybody about this. Willy sometimes signs himself out of the house at night but never actually leaves. He stays with me."

Goldie let out a breath of exasperation, shaking her head. "We need to know who's in the house at all times, Mrs. Volto. It's security protocol." She averted her eyes, embarrassed to have exposed their secret affair. "If you'd like Mr. Murphy to be your house guest, all you have to do is let us know. It's your home, after all."

"No!" Mrs. Volto was panicked. "I can't run the risk of Leonardo finding out about Willy and me. It would change everything."

By now, the buzzing outside had reached a high-pitched whine, a tinny pitch that couldn't be ignored.

"If you won't put Mr. Murphy's name on the official overnight guest list, then he can't stay here," Goldie said above the noise. "I'm sorry, but it's for his own safety. He could get shot as an intruder."

Mrs. Volto nodded, continuing to clutch the duvet to her neck. "I understand." She looked up at her lawyer. "You'll have to hide in my bathroom until the coast is clear and then sneak out. And we'll need to put an end to your overnight stays."

But Willy wasn't listening. Instead, he was gazing at the ceiling, one ear upturned, apparently distracted by the shrill buzz in the air.

"There's something outside," Goldie explained. "We're looking into it right now."

"What is it, Willy?" Mrs. Volto asked. "You look concerned."

"That sound is a drone," he said, pointing upward. "And it's hovering right over this house."

FOUR

Zeke stood on the lawn, gazing up at the dark sky, searching for the source of the noise.

"It's right there," Garth said, pointing at the roof. "Do you see it by the chimney?"

He swiveled. "Yeah, I see it."

There, hovering above the slate roof, was a drone. With four silver rotor blades sticking out from a black body, it had the appearance of a huge metal insect, menacing and dangerous. The buzz of the blades was cutting through the balmy night air like a swarm of angry bees, and Zeke watched it lift higher, wobbling slightly, as if someone was only just learning how to control it.

"We should look for the person piloting this thing," he said. "He's gotta be close."

Garth shook his head. "Actually, this drone has a range of about a mile, so the controller could be a lot farther away than you think." He looked over the hills, shrouded in darkness, possibly concealing all kinds of threats. "He could be watching us through binoculars. Or a sniper scope."

"We can't just let it fly around here," Zeke said. "It doesn't seem to have a weapon on it, but it could still be dangerous."

Neither man took his eyes off the drone as it slid down the roof tiles before launching into the air again and lurching to the left.

"We could try to shoot it down," Garth suggested. "If it stays still long enough."

Zeke didn't like that idea. "Karl mentioned that some of the neighbors are a little jittery after the gun attack. He doesn't want us to fire our weapons unless we have to."

"Well, it looks like we might have to." Garth pointed to a window, where a light shone through the drapes. The drone was hovering a few feet from the pane. "Isn't that Mrs. Volto's bedroom?"

"Yes, it is." Zeke saw a shape moving behind the drapes. "You stay here and I'll go upstairs." As he ran, he called out, "Don't try to shoot it. You might hit Mrs. Volto instead."

Rushing inside, Zeke took the stairs two at a time, finding Goldie at the top, gun in her hand, waiting for news.

"It's a drone," he said, eyes on the closed door of Mrs. Volto's room. "And it's right outside this bedroom. We need to get Mrs. Volto out, in case we have to shoot it down."

"Let's be respectful of her privacy," Goldie said. "I don't want to barge in again."

"Again?"

"Yeah, I went in there a couple minutes ago." She shook her head. "It doesn't matter."

Goldie knocked loudly on the door. "Mrs. Volto? Can we come in? It's important."

Zeke heard a door slam inside the room, then her voice call, "Yes, you can come in."

He wasted no time in entering the huge white-walled room, which had an enormous bed in the center. The noise of the drone was incessant, its outline visible behind the pulled drapes.

"Goldie, get Mrs. Volto out of here," he said, noticing their client standing next to the closed door of her bathroom, a silk robe tied above her stomach. "Take her to the panic room."

Mrs. Volto appeared hesitant, dithering by the bathroom door, hand hovering above the handle.

"Are you sure that's necessary?" she asked. "There's no danger, is there?"

"Not at the moment," he replied. "It's just a precaution until we deal with this drone. It can't hurt you, but it might be a distraction for something else."

"Okay." She remained steadfast. "It's just that…" She stopped. "Can't I go into my bathroom instead? It has a lock on the door."

"No." He looked at Goldie in confusion. "What's the problem here?"

"Mrs. Volto," Goldie said, going to join her. "You should be honest with Zeke. He's responsible for everybody's safety here, and he needs to know the situation." She then turned to him. "Willy Murphy is hiding in the bathroom. I discovered that he and Mrs. Volto are in a relationship, and she doesn't want anybody else to find out."

"Oh." This news wasn't exactly shocking to Zeke. He'd already spotted an intimacy between the lawyer and his client earlier that day, but an unauthorized overnight stay showed a flagrant disregard for the rules. "The FBI is here to keep you safe, Mrs. Volto, not to judge you. Take Willy into the panic room with you and we'll figure out a way to sneak him out of the house when this is over, and then I hope you'll stick to our security procedures."

A look of relief swept over Mrs. Volto's face as she was reassured that she could still guard her secret from the wider FBI team, and she opened the bathroom door. Willy stood on the tiles, barefoot in his suit, hair disheveled and a startled expression on his face.

Mrs. Volto took his hand. "You have to come into the panic room with me, Willy, but we'll get you out of the house when the coast is clear."

Zeke watched Willy edge his way through the door, eyes darting, hands twitching. He was nervous.

"That drone is spying on you, Louisa," he said, his gaze running across the covered window, where the shadow of the flying metal insect was hovering. "It's got to be Leonardo. We have to be more careful." He picked up his pace as the drone inched nearer. "Let's go. Quickly."

"I'll go with them," Goldie said, following them through the door. "Stay safe, Zeke. Okay?"

He smiled at her, pleasantly surprised at her genuine concern for him. "You too."

As soon as the door clicked shut behind them, Zeke turned to the window, raised his gun and threw the drapes aside. The drone was directly behind the pane, silver and black, four jutting legs topped with whizzing rotor blades. Zeke stood fast, aiming his gun at the bulbous body, scrutinizing the object, committing it to memory so he could identify it later.

That's when he noticed the small round camera attached to its back, the lens reflecting the light from the room. Willy had been right. This drone was a spy, sent to record images of the house or, more specifically, to record images of Mrs. Volto. Perhaps her husband had begun to suspect an affair. If that were true, Louisa was in more danger than she realized, because Mafia men did not like to be humiliated. And Louisa's running around with Willy Murphy would certainly humiliate a tough guy like Leonardo Volto.

Zeke edged to the window, flipped the catch and pushed it open. For a second there was a tense standoff, the drone hovering just a few feet away, creating a breeze that ruffled his hair. He wondered if he might be able to grab the camera from the metal body. There could be footage of the launch site on there, and maybe, just maybe, the perp had recorded his own face in the process. As Zeke reached out to touch it with a hand, it jerked away, sudden and sharp. Then it was gone, disappearing up into the sky, its buzzing fading on the wind.

Zeke closed the window, fastened the latch and stood in the welcome silence that was descending. The appearance of that drone had unsettled him. Leonardo Volto was a brutal and cruel man, obsessed with a bizarre Mafia code of honor. If he somehow managed to secure recorded evidence of his wife's cheating, he would likely go to untold lengths to restore his honor, even if it meant harming his unborn child in the process.

What was more, Goldie could find herself not only facing danger from bounty hunters, but also caught up in the cross fire of an attack from Leonardo. She was now doubly at risk, and that meant Zeke would have to stay close to her at all times. No matter how fractured their relationship, they had to stick together to defeat the escalating risks.

Goldie, yet again, paced in her bedroom, going stir-crazy, closing her eyes in an attempt to conjure up images of wide open fields and endless blue sky. Instead of the usual birdsong she enjoyed from the yard, all she could hear was the sound of hammering as workmen constructed a new fence behind the pool, much higher than the previous one and topped with barbed wire. When completed, this place would look like a prison. And as far as Goldie was concerned, it *was* a prison. Due to Karl's concerns about signals

being tracked, her cell phone had been confiscated, and the only reading material in the
house were Mrs. Volto's interior design magazines that Goldie found shallow and dull. The
walls of her room had become a cell, and she
knew every single hairline crack and dent in
the paintwork. She knew exactly how many
pebbles were in the seascape painting on the
wall and how many flowers on her patterned
duvet. With no natural light allowed into the
house, Goldie was slowly turning mad, with
no distraction from the jumbled mess of
thoughts and regrets in her head. Years ago,
she would've turned to her faith for comfort,
but she'd lost the ability to pray, assuming
that the previous channel she'd had with God
was now shut down for good.

There was a knock on the door, and she
knew it was Zeke. Only he had bothered to
check on her all morning, bringing her a
snack and a drink and updating her on the
progress of the work in the yard.

She walked to the door and turned the key
in the lock, opening up just a crack to see
Zeke's smiling face.

"Hi," he said. "Can I come in?"

She opened the door wide. "Sure. Come
join the party. It's just getting started."

He laughed, closing the door behind him and turning the key.

"Do I really have to be locked in here?" she asked. "It's so claustrophobic."

"Karl says it's necessary," Zeke replied. "He doesn't want to run the risk of any of the contractors walking in here and seeing you."

"Like that's gonna happen," she said exasperatedly. "Nobody on the team would allow strangers to wander all over the house."

He shrugged. "Karl says it's the rule, and he's so stressed today that I don't want to challenge him on anything." He sat on the bed. "He's concerned that the mole might've passed on information regarding Mrs. Volto's movements in the house, giving him the perfect moment to launch the drone."

Goldie was skeptical. "It was really late, Zeke. It would've been easy to predict that Mrs. Volto would be in her bedroom at that time, and any Mafia member who's familiar with the house would know which room is hers."

"That's what I said, but Karl is running checks on all agents and police guards. Again."

"I guess this attack has got him worked up, huh?"

"Technically, it wasn't an attack," Zeke said. "It was a reconnaissance mission."

"Do you think Leonardo knows about his wife and Willy?"

"I think he's suspicious. Mrs. Volto said that Marsha didn't come here to kill her, but they had a conversation and ended up arguing."

Goldie could see where Zeke might be heading. "It looks like Leonardo sent Marsha here to find out if she was having an affair with Willy."

"That sounds like the most likely explanation to me. If Mrs. Volto admitted the affair to Marsha, that would certainly make her angry, right? What did Marsha call Mrs. Volto during her attack?"

Goldie cast her mind back. "A dirty rotten liar."

"I think we did the right thing in allowing Willy to sneak away without being seen last night. If Leonardo finds out about this relationship, he'll probably try to kill her."

"But Mrs. Volto is so sure that her husband would never put their baby's life in jeopardy."

Zeke raised his eyebrows. "What if the baby isn't Leonardo's?"

Goldie gasped. "You think it's Willy's baby?"

"It's plausible. We don't know how long the

affair has been going on. And if Leonardo suspects the child isn't his, he might not be inclined to protect his wife anymore."

Goldie sat heavily in the chair in the corner. "That's why she's so terrified of him finding out. She knows he'd kill her."

"You and I have to promise not to tell this secret," Zeke said. "I don't usually like secrets, but this one might be the only thing keeping Mrs. Volto alive."

"I promise." Goldie looked down into her hands. The bond of a shared secret was powerful, and she felt it cement them together right at that moment. "Listen, Zeke. I appreciate you taking care of me these last couple days. You're the only one who's bothered to check on me when I'm shut up in here." She laughed awkwardly. "I think I'd have died from dehydration without you bringing me drinks. So, thank you. You're okay. I mean, you're a good guy. Mostly."

"Wow," he said, throwing her a big, beaming smile. "You're almost as bad at giving praise as you are at receiving it."

"Shut up," she said playfully. "Praise is not my strong point."

He sat up straight. "Can I ask you something, Goldie?"

"Sure."

"Do you like yourself?"

She stiffened. "What does that have to do with anything?"

"I'm sorry if I'm being a little personal, but you're kind of down on yourself."

She rose and walked to the window to stand in front of the closed blinds and imagine the beautiful rolling hills behind them.

"I try to be a nice person and care for others, but I always feel like a part of me is missing." She placed a flat hand on her chest. "I can't ever truly like myself while I'm incomplete." She turned. "Does that make sense?"

He was gazing at her, giving her his rapt attention. "It makes more sense than you know."

She always assumed that the hole in her heart could've been filled by a husband and family, but now she wasn't so sure. She was smart enough to have worked out that true happiness could not be gleaned from another person. If she could marry happiness, she'd have done it long ago. Whatever she was missing went a lot deeper than that.

"I like to keep busy," she said. "That way, I don't have to think about it too much."

Zeke nodded slowly. "I hear you. Sometimes it's hard to be still."

"Well, somebody sure is forcing me to be

still right now," she said, gesturing to the room around her. "Because there are no distractions in here."

"After you disappeared, I found it hard to be still too." He stared at the floor. "Every time the telephone rang, I'd jump up and race to answer it. I just kept on hoping that you'd have gotten our new number somehow."

"I tried, Zeke."

"I know, but for some reason, it just wasn't meant to be."

She laughed. "That's a pretty convenient excuse, huh?"

"There has to be good reason why we were kept apart, Goldie," he said. "What happened was for the best, I'm sure of it."

"It's so easy to explain away bad things by claiming that God's in control or that it's meant to be." She crossed her arms. "It means that we never have to take responsibility for our actions. We can behave in any cruel way we like while claiming that God has it all in hand. It's such an easy excuse."

"That's not what's happening here," he said. "I was never cruel toward you."

She narrowed her eyes. Zeke's failure to apologize certainly felt like cruelty to her.

"If it's all the same to you, I'd rather you didn't use God to justify your failings," she said. "It wasn't God who destroyed my letters. It wasn't God who changed your telephone number and it sure wasn't God who decided to move all the way to New York without considering me at all." She pointed at him. "Moving away from the only place I could find you was definitely your fault, so casually telling me that God's in control simply doesn't cut it."

He rubbed his chin, a pained expression on his face. "My parents did the wrong thing by trying to prevent contact with you. They didn't understand the harm they were doing at the time, but I choose to forgive them and I hope you can do the same one day. What I'm trying to say is that God can work bad things for His purpose. There is meaning in what happened to us because He can make it so."

"There's no meaning in suffering, Zeke, at least none that I can see."

"That's because you're looking with human eyes. Faith is often hard, Goldie. It's like stepping into the darkness and holding out your hand, waiting for someone you can't see to reach out and take it." He smiled. "Sometimes it feels like you're standing there in the dark forever before you can feel those comforting fingers grip yours."

"Yeah, well, I've been waiting twenty-one years and my hand is still empty, so I hope you'll understand why I gave up." She shrugged. "God doesn't want to hold my hand."

"That's not true."

"Let's drop the subject, huh?" She was tired and lethargic, partly from inertia, partly from emotional overload. "How long until I can leave this room?"

"I'll just go check on the yard work and get another update, but I figure the fence will be done in about an hour." He stood and walked across the carpet. "Remember to keep the door locked."

She sighed, following him. "Yeah, I know. I can't be seen or heard."

He slipped through the door and she turned the key, resting her forehead on the wood, eyes closed and mood low. She needed to get out of this room, with its four walls closing in on her. Zeke said that the work might only take another hour. She could last another hour. Maybe she'd miscounted the flowers on her duvet. She could start over again.

With a big sigh, she secured her hair with a tie from her wrist and headed for the bed, noticing a thick red book lying on the top. It hadn't been there before Zeke's visit, so he must've left it there, almost certainly on purpose.

Turning over the book, she grimaced. Typical Zeke. He had left her a pocket Bible, thinking that all she needed was God's word to make everything better. She picked it up, tracing the bold embossed lettering on the front, feeling a shiver enter her spine. Zeke was trying to be kind, but the gesture felt patronizing. And it wouldn't make a difference, of course, because she would never open the pages, so it was a wasted effort.

Opening the drawer of her bedside dresser, she slipped the Bible inside and ran her eyes across the flowers on her duvet.

"One, two, three…"

Zeke stirred honey into chamomile tea on the kitchen counter. Mrs. Volto was due to give her first day of testimony in court the following day, and she was supernervous. Since the drone incident, she had become jumpy and easily spooked, which could impede her ability to be a strong and reliable witness.

"Hey there."

He turned to see Goldie performing a running slide into the kitchen dressed in jeans and an oversize hoodie. The central air had developed a fault, stuck on a high setting, so she'd put on some fluffy purple socks, enabling her to easily slip across the tiles of the floor.

"Hi," he said. "You seem happy."

"I'm just so glad to be out of that room. Even this dark and dingy house seems like a playground after five hours in a box."

"Yeah, the blackout takes some getting used to," he said. "It's a little creepy, huh?"

She took a mug from the overhead shelf and flipped the kettle to boil. "Yes, it is. I keep expecting to see Morticia Addams gliding down the stairs."

He wondered whether she would mention the Bible he'd left on her bed, but she said nothing. Filling her cup with boiling water, she dropped in a fruit tea bag and began to stir, her gaze settled in the middle distance. She was standing close to him, so close he could detect a coconut scent on her hair, which was piled up in a messy bun, tendrils falling over her face. Her proximity was having a physical effect on him, and his heart beat much faster than normal. No matter how hard he tried, he was unable to control his powerful reaction to her.

"Karl has requested the delivery of a drone jammer from headquarters," he said. "That will block the signal and put a stop to any more flying activity."

"That's great."

He picked up the chamomile tea from the counter. "I guess I'd better take this to Mrs. Volto. She needs something to calm her down."

Goldie smiled. "Should I make a start on dinner? I think it's supposed to be Garth's turn tonight, but he's had a busy day."

"Sure. Why not?" He made no attempt to move away, enjoying the sensation of being next to her. "I'll help out too."

"Thank you."

They stood in silence for a few seconds as Goldie continued to stir her tea, her spoon clinking slowly around the mug. Zeke placed his palm flat on the counter and let it rest there, just a little way from Goldie's. Slowly but surely, she inched her fingers toward his until their tips were touching, just lightly, but definite contact.

"That tea won't deliver itself to Mrs. Volto," she said quietly. "It'll get cold."

"Yeah." He hesitated. "Can I say something first?"

She took the spoon from the mug, placed it on the counter and shifted her body to face his. With only a tiny gap between them, he was jolted by the close-up of her eyes, emerald green with an edge of hazel, perhaps the most beautiful eyes he'd ever seen.

"I…um… I know it's been hard to adjust," he stammered. "Neither of us expected to see each other again, and our history makes everything complicated."

She nodded. "It was a shock to the system to see you out of the blue like that." She took a deep, steadying breath. "It's been like falling into icy cold water and struggling to breathe."

"I really did love you," he said, feeling an overwhelming need to say it. "You know that, right?"

"I want to believe it, Zeke." There was a hardness to her voice. "But if you loved me, you'd never have given up on me."

He quashed his frustrations. "If you don't stop holding on to this bitterness, you'll never be happy."

"I wish you'd just say sorry and let me move on. Why do you have to be so stubborn?"

"The only person who owes you an apology is your father. I think you're projecting all your frustrations at him onto me."

She tilted her head, as if giving it some thought. "Maybe," she said finally. "But he's not here, is he? You are. And you could at least try to make me feel better by acknowledging your part in my pain."

Zeke knew that giving Goldie a false apology would make him resent her, possibly even destroy the chance of a friendship. Having already experienced this type of injustice, he knew the ramifications. It would chip away at him, just like the situation with Susan had chipped away at him, until he had to get as far away from her as possible.

"You're right about the tea," he said, stepping away. "It's getting cold." He headed for the door. "I'll come back to help with dinner."

"Zeke," she called. "Just a minute."

He stopped.

"You left a Bible on my bed," she said. "But I didn't ask you for one."

"I thought you might find it comforting. Did you open it up?"

"No."

"Why don't you try?" he asked. "It's what you need, I promise."

She turned to the counter, back to the quiet, slow stirring of her cup.

"It must be nice up there on your high horse," she said. "Be careful you don't fall off."

With a deep sigh, he accepted defeat and left the room.

* * *

Goldie tossed and turned in her bed, punching the pillow and huffing in frustration. Sleep simply would not come that night. She eyed the clock on her dresser—1:35 a.m. The whole house was quiet and still, with just the occasional faint sound of footsteps downstairs, where Angela was patrolling on the first half of the nightduty shift.

She sat up and swung her legs over the side of the bed. What was the point in lying awake, unable to stop herself thinking of Zeke and his broad, heart-fluttering smile? All it did was upset her. He had tried hard to keep their conversation light and friendly while cooking dinner earlier on, but it had ended up being awkward and strained. Maybe he had a valid point regarding her frustration at her father. Perhaps she *was* projecting the anger onto Zeke instead. But she hated to admit to herself that Zeke might be right. It could bring her defenses tumbling down.

"I gotta get out of here," she muttered, standing up to pull on sweatpants and a hoodie over her pajamas. "I'm going crazy. I'm even talking to myself."

Creeping to the door, she turned the key in the lock and stepped out onto the landing. The hush of nighttime enveloped her like a blanket and she padded along the carpet, hand on the banister. She'd just get herself a cup of tea and watch some television to wait for drowsiness to come. There was bound to be an old movie on one of the channels.

When she reached the kitchen, she filled a glass with water, clicked the kettle to boil and placed a couple of cookies on a plate. While sipping the water, she heard the whoosh of drapes being thrown aside in the hallway and the patio door being opened.

"Who's there?" she called, placing the glass on the counter. "Angela? Is that you?"

She peeked around the door, immediately seeing the patio door wide open, allowing the cool nighttime breeze into the house. And a dark figure was rushing down the path, head bent and shoulders hunched, as if upset.

"Angela?" she called again. "Are you here? Somebody just went outside."

She heard the sounds of running water in the downstairs bathroom and realized that Angela must be taking a comfort break. So who had opened the door and ventured outside at this hour of the night? And why?

Goldie pushed her feet into Zeke's sneakers and lifted a pale blue coat from a hook by the door, making sure to pull up the hood and push all her red curls inside. If she was meant to be in hiding, she should take extra care to obscure her most recognizable feature, even at this late and quiet hour.

The pool area was beautiful at night, with bright white lights shining through the aquamarine water. Set in the center of a wonderfully neat lawn, this environment should have the power to make anyone blissfully happy. Yet here in the midst of it all was Mrs. Volto, sitting on a pool lounger in a bathrobe, weeping into a tissue.

"Mrs. Volto," Goldie said, approaching with a gentle voice. "What on earth are you doing outside? You know you can't come out here without an agent. Please come indoors."

Mrs. Volto looked up at her with red-tinged eyes framed by perfectly groomed brows.

"I just wanted some air," she said, running her eyes up and down Goldie's attire. "Why are you bundled up like that? That's my raincoat."

"I'm incognito," she said, sitting next to Mrs. Volto on the lounger. "There's a hit on me, remember?"

"Ah, yes. The color suits you." Mrs. Volto smiled weakly. "Please have it. My husband bought it for me, so I have no desire to keep it." She began to cry again, wiping her cheeks with the tissue. "I'm sorry. I keep thinking about having to face him in court."

Goldie placed a comforting hand on her back. "It's natural to be nervous, but try not to worry. Just tell the truth and you can't go wrong."

Mrs. Volto suddenly let out a cry, rather like a kitten mewing, and clutched Goldie's hand. "I'm scared, Agent Simmons. Leonardo has wanted a child for years and years, so I knew he'd never harm me while I was pregnant. But if he finds out about Willy and me, it would change everything."

Now seemed like an opportune time to ask a pertinent question. "Is this your husband's baby?" she asked. "Or is it Willy's?"

"It's Leonardo's," Mrs. Volto replied quickly. "Willy and I have only been in a relationship for four months, so it can't possibly be his." She placed a hand on her stomach protectively. "Marsha came here to find out how the pregnancy was progressing. Leonardo sent her to get some sonogram pictures."

"Did she suspect you were having an affair? Is that why you two argued?"

Mrs. Volto squirmed uncomfortably on the lounger.

"Yes," she said finally. "She accused me of cheating on Leonardo and of being pregnant with another man's child. You see, Leo and I were married for ten years with no sign of a baby, so he's naturally suspicious that within two weeks of him being charged, I announced I was six weeks pregnant." She laughed sardonically. "It does sound a little too convenient, doesn't it?"

"Yes, it does," Goldie said. "But if you say that your baby is your husband's, then I believe you."

Mrs. Volto squeezed her hand. "Thank you." She dried her eyes and shoved the tissue into the pocket of her robe. "That means a lot to me."

"Now, let's go inside. Zeke will go crazy when he finds out we've both broken the rules."

"Zeke?" Mrs. Volto put a finger to her lips and tapped. "He's the tall, handsome one, right? The one who looks at you like you're the most beautiful creature he ever saw."

Goldie shook her head. "Stop. He looks at me the same way he looks at everybody else."

"Do you really think so?" Mrs. Volto side-eyed her. "In the middle of all this gloom and danger, I enjoy watching the two of you skirting around each other. It's sweet."

"We do not skirt around each other," Goldie protested. "We're just working some things out."

Mrs. Volto laughed heartily, showing her perfect teeth. "Well, I wish you'd work them out a little quicker, because I'm getting impatient for the happy ending."

"There's no happy ending for us, so don't get your hopes up." She tugged on the sleeve of Mrs. Volto's robe. "Now can we please go inside?" She glanced at the high metal fence that surrounded them. "I'm getting nervous out here."

Goldie helped the pregnant woman to stand, and Mrs. Volto let out a gasp, gripping her wrist tightly.

"What's that noise?" she asked, suddenly beginning to hurry along the path. "It sounds like another drone. We have to get inside!"

But Goldie had no time to react because the bulky body of the drone appeared as if from nowhere, rising above the fence like a robotic spider and setting them in its sights. And she'd forgotten to bring her gun.

"Run!" Goldie yelled, picking up a stone from the nearby rock garden to hurl at the menacing hulk of metal flying their way. "Go get Zeke."

Mrs. Volto raced to the door, leaving Goldie alone. She could do nothing but grab the rest of the decorative stones and one by one throw them at the drone with all her might, giving Mrs. Volto the opportunity to safely slip through the door. When her supply of rocks was exhausted, the drone hovered between her and the house, cutting off her route to safety. That's when she noticed a package of some sort strapped to the metal body, trailing wires, a cell phone taped to the side.

"Oh no," she said, turning to run. "It's a bomb."

FIVE

The high security fence loomed large, blocking Goldie's only means of escape. With no way around it, she had no choice but to go over. Heart hammering in her chest, she picked up her pace and took a flying leap onto a stray pool lounger, using it like a springboard to launch herself at the wall. Her fingertips just managed to grip the edge while Zeke's sneakers squeaked on the metal bars as she scrambled to throw her body across the top. The barbs on the wire dug into the flesh beneath her jeans, tearing the fabric, but she pulled and yanked herself free, leaving the blue coat dangling on the spikes as she dropped heavily to the ground on the other side. Winded but pumped full of adrenaline, she jumped up, ready to flee.

With her hair flowing in the breeze, she ran blindly in the dark, over the uneven ground of the field, struggling to keep a sure footing in her oversize shoes. The noise of the drone was incessant, whining, almost singing, and hot on her heels. There was no way she could outrun this thing. She could only hope something or someone would come to her aid.

"Please, Lord," she muttered. "I know I don't deserve it, but help me."

She hit a hole in the ground, turned her ankle and cried out in pain, falling hard on the scrubby grass. Before she knew what was happening, she was tumbling over and over as she hit a slope, bumping on stones and clods of earth, feeling her body absorb an assortment of blows. The buzz was horribly loud, the drone directly overhead, just waiting for her to come to a standstill. Then it would crash land onto her, blowing her skyhigh.

Covering her eyes, not wanting to watch her own death unfold, Goldie waited for the inevitable. Yet the explosion never came. Instead, a gunshot pierced the night, cutting through the buzz and echoing across the hills. Someone was shooting. Another shot rang out and, opening her eyes, she saw the drone spark from contact with the bullet. The metal body wobbled, its buzz erratic, the operator clearly losing control of its flight. As if in slow motion, she watched the drone spin like a dying fly, spluttering and jerking, until it crashed to the ground about a hundred feet away and exploded with a bang. She shielded her face from the hot, rushing wind by burying her head in a bent elbow.

"Goldie!" Zeke was yelling out her name. "Where are you? Talk to me."

"I'm here," she yelled back. "I'm okay. I think."

She pushed herself up to stand but groaned in pain as soon as her ankle bore her weight. She fell onto her behind, her body aching with the punishment of the blows she'd taken.

In a matter of seconds, Zeke was there, lifting her up, carrying her in his arms, taking her away from the burning drone, back toward the safety of the house. She snaked her arms around his neck, taking solace in his strength, grateful that he had come to her rescue so quickly.

"Thank you," she said weakly, her adrenaline diminishing. "That was close."

"We need to get you checked for injuries," he said, his face stony. "You got a cut lip there."

She brought a hand to her mouth and checked her fingers, wiping the blood on her pants. What she really wanted to do right now was close her eyes and sleep. After hours of infuriating insomnia, now was the moment her body chose to succumb to slumber, while she rested in Zeke's arms. She must be in shock.

As he walked, Zeke winced and sucked air through his teeth, and Goldie glanced down to see his bare feet walking on the thistly ground.

"You're not wearing any shoes," she said. "You need shoes."

"I know." He winked at her. "But somebody took my sneakers."

The atmosphere in the room was tense and Zeke was wide-awake and wired, eager to discuss the recent drone attack. Christina had decided to hold an immediate emergency meeting, despite the time approaching 3:30 a.m. She and Karl had driven from their respective homes without delay, alarmed by this latest development in the Volto case.

Christina welcomed each person in the room: Zeke, Goldie, Angela and Karl. Mrs. Volto's home cinema room had been deemed the best option for this meeting. With no windows and excellent soundproofing, they were not only safe from attack, but Mrs. Volto's sleep wouldn't be disturbed by their voices. Come what may, she would be attending court later that day and had taken a prescribed sedative to calm her nerves.

"Garth won't be attending this meeting," Christina said, opening her briefcase. "He's standing guard outside Mrs. Volto's room. But he and Angela need to get some sleep before escorting her to court this afternoon, so let's be quick and to the point." She turned to Angela, eyes blazing. "How on earth did Mrs. Volto bypass you and manage to slip outside unseen?"

Angela was sheepish. "I was in the bathroom. I didn't see her."

"The CCTV footage recorded Mrs. Volto and Agent Simmons talking outside for at least fifteen minutes. And you were unaware of this lapse in security the entire time. If you need to spend fifteen minutes in the bathroom, you should wake up Agent Cooper to take your place. Is that clear?"

"Um… I needed to take an urgent phone call," Angela stammered. "It was personal and I didn't want anybody to overhear."

Christina was clearly unhappy. "More urgent than protecting a witness in a Mafia trial?"

"I'm sorry ma'am," Angela said. "It won't happen again."

Christina sighed, pinched the bridge of her

nose. "The prosecutor for the Volto case tells me that Mrs. Volto's testimony is vital in persuading the jury to return a guilty verdict. We absolutely cannot allow anything to happen to her, or to her baby. I'm disappointed that we slipped up again." She opened a notebook and began to write inside. "You'll be issued a formal warning, Agent Martin, and another slip like this will be grounds for instant dismissal from the case. Do I make myself clear?"

"Yes, ma'am."

"Go turn in for the night. We'll take over from here."

Angela rose from her seat. "Thank you, ma'am. Good night."

Christina watched and waited until the agent clicked the door closed behind her.

"We can't discount the possibility that Angela deliberately allowed Mrs. Volto to go outside," she said. "We knew that someone was leaking information about the case, and Angela could be a perfect fit."

"That doesn't make sense," Zeke said. "Marsha got hold of that classified schedule before Angela was even assigned to the case."

"Well, somebody must've told the drone operator that Mrs. Volto was outside, giving him the ideal opportunity to attack." Christina stood and began to pace, as if thinking hard to put the pieces together. "The parts of the exploded drone are being gathered by a forensics team right now, but early indications suggest there was no camera on it. That means it was being guided by sight alone."

"That means somebody was watching," Karl said.

"Exactly," Christina added. "He was close by, able to determine the exact time to strike. Whoever was controlling that drone knew Mrs. Volto was sitting by the pool and took the opportunity to try to eliminate her. Our tech guys are installing the drone jamming technology right now, so at least we won't face another attack like this one."

Zeke couldn't believe that Christina could be so shortsighted. Did she really think that Mrs. Volto was the target of this improvised bomb?

"The drone didn't chase Mrs. Volto," Zeke said. "It was trying to eliminate Goldie."

Christina glanced at Karl, as if they had both been expecting this claim from him.

"Goldie was wearing quite a distinctive coat that belongs to Mrs. Volto," Christina said. "In the dark and with the hood up, it makes total sense that the drone operator would chase that blue coat. The perp is probably associated with the Mafia and has seen Mrs. Volto wearing it before."

Zeke looked at Goldie stretched out, exhausted in her seat, her curls cascading over her shoulders.

"The coat got caught on the barbed wire," he said. "And Goldie slipped out of it. The drone continued to chase her, even though her hair was clearly visible."

Karl wasn't convinced of the theory. "Like Christina already said, it was dark and visibility was poor. Perhaps the drone operator was only able to see an outline of a person once Goldie was over the fence. That field on the other side of the yard is pitch-black."

"I'm not buying it." Zeke shook his head. "I want to agree with you, because I'd like Goldie to stay here where I can protect her, but it's getting too dangerous. She needs to be moved."

Again, Christina and Karl exchanged a knowing glance, and Zeke didn't like their unspoken words.

"Listen, Zeke," Karl began awkwardly. "Your history with Goldie might be clouding your judgment a little. You two are close, perhaps too close."

"We're not close, sir, not at all."

Goldie was in agreement. "Zeke's right.

We have history, but it's all been left firmly in the past."

"What do you think, Goldie?" Karl asked. "Do you think the drone was targeting you?"

She shrugged. "I honestly don't know what to think anymore. It's possible that I was the intended target, but I can't be sure."

"The drone that exploded a couple hours ago was a different drone from the one spying on Mrs. Volto yesterday," Zeke said. "It was a different size and color and shape." He rubbed a hand across his mousy blond curls. "I know this may sound crazy, but I don't think the two drones are linked. The first drone came to spy on Mrs. Volto, but the second one came to kill Goldie. They were probably being piloted by different people."

"You're right, Zeke," Karl said with a smile. "You *do* sound crazy."

"Think about it," he said. "The first drone didn't make any attempt to hurt Mrs. Volto, even though it could've crashed through her bedroom window at any time. It only wanted to record images. We know that her husband hasn't ordered a hit on her, but it looks like he might want to spy on her."

"Why would he do that?" Karl asked.

Zeke had already assured Mrs. Volto that

her secret was safe with him, and he wasn't about to betray her by revealing her affair.

"I don't know. Maybe he wants to see his baby getting bigger. Mr. Volto may be a hardened criminal, but that doesn't mean he can't be a doting father."

Karl took off his glasses and breathed on a lens before cleaning it. "Let's be realistic here. The first drone was a reconnaissance mission, casing the house and lawns. The second drone used that information to launch the attack. It makes much more sense than your theory."

"But the two drones were totally different," Zeke argued. "If it's the same guy, why wouldn't he use the same one?"

"Are you sure the drones were different?" Karl replied. "One big metal fly looks very much like another as far as I'm concerned, especially in the dark."

"No, sir," Zeke said. "They were definitely different."

Christina interjected. "It's clear that you're concerned about Goldie, Zeke, and you're doing a great job taking care of her. From what I understand, you cleaned her wounds and checked her over after the incident, and your attentiveness has been noted."

Zeke raised an eyebrow. "Why do I sense

that the word *however* is about to be un-
leashed?"

"However," Christina said emphatically,
"all the signs point toward Mrs. Volto being
the subject of both the gun attack and the
drone bomb. Even if her husband didn't order
the hit, somebody is clearly trying to eliminate Louisa Volto, and Goldie has simply
been caught in the cross fire."

Zeke didn't agree, not in the slightest, but
what was the point of arguing? Christina and
Karl would only accuse him of allowing his
personal feelings to sway his professional
opinion.

Karl checked his watch. "Zeke, I'll be taking over the nighttime guard duty in a half
hour. And I've decided to move into the house
until the trial is over. Can you tell Garth to go
to bed at 4:00 a.m., please? And I want you
to keep a close eye on Goldie in case there's
a concussion."

"Yes, sir."

"Why don't we make some coffee, Karl,
and get started on the incident report." Christina rose from her seat. "There's a lot to do,
but let's do it quietly. Mrs. Volto has a big
day ahead."

Zeke watched them leave, heads together
in a hushed whisper, and he let his body sink

further into the soft leather chair. Meanwhile, Goldie was blinking slowly, apparently relaxed, as if on the verge of sleep.

"You have to be more careful, Goldie," he said. "I'm certain that a bounty hunter is on to you, and I'm worried that Angela might be involved."

"You could be right," she said. "But Karl and Christina think your judgment is clouded because of our relationship."

"That's not true," he retorted, before considering the idea more carefully. "At least, I don't think it's true." He had to be honest here. "I must admit that my feelings for you are complicated, but I don't think it's affecting my judgment."

He had clearly engaged her interest, as she pushed on her flat palms to slide herself upright.

"Your feelings are complicated?" she queried. "How so?"

Zeke wasn't sure he could summon the right words to explain exactly how he felt, because, in truth, he wasn't even sure of his feelings himself.

"I like you, Goldie," he said. "I like you a lot, much more than I should considering we're partners. I need to put some emotional distance between us, because I'm falling—"

He stopped. "I'm falling out of step with the assignment. I could see that Mrs. Volto was restless before bed last night, and I should've asked her if she was okay."

"Your assignment is me, Zeke," she said. "Mrs. Volto's safety is on Garth and Angela now."

"Yeah, well, I'm not doing such a great job of being your protector either. That's the second close call you've had since you've been in hiding."

"I'm not an easy person to guard," she said sheepishly. "I shouldn't have gone outside, so don't be too hard on yourself."

"I'm so glad you're okay. When that explosion ripped into the sky, I was terrified. I mean, I've been scared before, but not like that."

Zeke's tight chest was still recovering from the terror, from the fear that he had lost her all over again. It had made him question how deep his feelings truly ran.

She smiled, lifted up her leg to focus on her swollen ankle. "Apart from the sprain and a few scratches, I'm totally fine."

"I wouldn't say you're totally fine," Zeke said. "In fact, you're dealing with a lot of issues."

"Yeah, but that's my problem, not yours."

"I've been trying to help."

Goldie snorted. "By whitewashing the past?"

"I'm not whitewashing anything," he protested. "You seem determined to place the blame on me instead of accepting that we're both victims of circumstance."

"Circumstance?" She seemed incredulous. "Is that what you call it when you can't be bothered to track down the girl you love?"

He sighed. "I don't want to go there again, Goldie. It's too late and I'm too tired."

She stood up, balancing on one leg. "That's fine by me. I'm going to bed."

He jumped up to slide his arm around her back, tucking his hand into her armpit. "Let me help. You can't get upstairs alone."

She leaned on him, limping awkwardly to the door.

"This would be a lot quicker and easier if I carried you," he said.

"That's never gonna happen again," she said, continuing to hobble. "I'm not a helpless princess, Zeke. I can take care of myself."

He smiled, although it was not a smile of happiness. Goldie's defensiveness was maddening. She claimed that she didn't need anything or anybody, not even God's grace. And she would never let up on her pressure to win an apology from him, to be the one in the right and prove to herself that she was the wronged party.

This cemented his belief that some emotional distance was definitely required.

Goldie towel dried her hair as she limped downstairs, her head fuzzy after the very late night. Despite sleeping until 11:00 a.m., she was still groggy and bleary-eyed as she headed in the direction of nearby voices, taking care to bear most of her weight on her good ankle.

"Good morning," she said, entering the darkened room and seeing paperwork spread across the new coffee table, a replacement for the one destroyed by the shooter. "Mrs. Volto, how are you feeling today?"

Mrs. Volto stood abruptly and placed a flat palm on her chest. "Oh, Goldie, you scared me. I didn't hear you coming. Willy and I were just doing some last minute preparations before I go to court this afternoon."

Her lawyer sat on the sofa, languishing with an elbow propped up on the armrest. "Louisa is understandably nervous after what happened with the exploding drone." He regarded Goldie with a mixture of curiosity and contempt. "How many more times will my client be put at risk by the sloppy security provided by the FBI?"

"Stop it, Willy," Mrs. Volto admonished. "It was Goldie who was injured in the attack, not me. You can see she's struggling to walk."

Willy's gaze traveled to Goldie's foot, held an inch off the ground, while she leaned against the wall, the towel now resting across her shoulders.

"Agent Simmons is trained in close, personal protection," he said dryly. "That means she should be able to mitigate the risks. Going outside with no gun and no means of defense was foolhardy, and you could've been killed, Lousia."

"I guess you'll be asking for more money, huh?" Goldie said. "It's always about the money with you, isn't it?"

"Someone is sending bombs raining down on my client's property," he said, eyeballing her. "And that makes me nervous. It also makes me wonder exactly how much money she's going to need to make any necessary repairs to her house and yard. Only money can give her the best quality of life, so please excuse me for trying to secure the best possible deal."

Mrs. Volto, wearing a black jersey dress, walked to Goldie and took her hand. Her baby bump stretched across the fabric, making the dress ride up at the hem. For all her money, Goldie figured that Mrs. Volto could buy some decent maternity clothes, but maybe this was all part of the plan. A scared pregnant woman in a badly fitted dress would surely invoke the sympathies of the jury.

"The drone bomb wasn't intended for me," Mrs. Volto said to her. "I'm not the one in serious danger here. You are."

Willy stood up and carefully smoothed the creases from his suit jacket. "Both Agent Cooper and Agent Phillips believe that these attacks are aimed at you, Louisa, so let's not openly contradict them. Agent Cooper has his ear to the ground, and his informants all say the same thing—the bounty hunters have swallowed the story about Agent Simmons hiding out in New Mexico." A wide smile spread across his face as Garth, himself, walked through the door with Zeke. "And here's the man himself. I was just explaining to my client that Agent Simmons is perfectly safe here, isn't that right?"

"I believe so," Garth replied. "My underworld contacts are rarely wrong about these things."

"Well, they're wrong this time," Mrs. Volto

muttered, too quietly for anybody but Goldie to hear. "Because that thing wasn't chasing me."

Goldie smiled, squeezed her hand, and an understanding passed between them, perhaps even crossing a line into friendship. In a surprising turn of events, it would appear that Mrs. Volto was becoming her ally.

"If I can do anything to help, just let me know," Mrs. Volto whispered. "Once the trial is over, I have plenty of money to employ our own security guards." Without turning her head, she slid her eyes over to Garth. "Ones we can truly trust."

"Thank you for the offer," Goldie whispered back. "But I don't think it's necessary."

"We'll be leaving for court in one hour," Garth said, adjusting the tie on his dark and somber suit. "So if you have any last minute preparations, you may want to do them now."

"Some tea is in order," Willy said, taking Mrs. Volto's hand and heading to the kitchen. "To banish those jitters."

"I'll go wake Angela," Garth said, turning to leave. "She's not on the ball this morning."

Goldie put a steadying hand on Zeke's shoulder and used him as a crutch, hopping to the armchair and lowering herself into it, raising her foot to rest it gingerly on the low table.

"Angela is playing with fire by oversleeping like this," she said. "It makes me wonder whether she's really committed to doing a good job here."

"That's my worry too," Zeke said, sitting on the coffee table to be as close as possible. "I've been considering the possibility that she accessed the Volto records before being assigned to the case. Even though she was in New York at the time of Marsha's attack, she might've used her high-level clearance to take a look at the case files and sell them to the Mafia."

Goldie thought of Angela, of her tendency to put her foot in her mouth and her sometimes ditzy ways. "My gut tells me she's not betraying us. She might be a sloppy agent, but she's not a traitor."

"So how did the drone operator know when to strike?" Zeke asked. "How did he know that it was you out there in Mrs. Volto's blue coat? How does he know you never left Pennsylvania, but stayed right here in Gladwyne?"

"I don't know, Zeke. We have no concrete evidence that I was even the target." She checked around the door and dropped her voice. "Although even Mrs. Volto now thinks that the attacker is a bounty hunter looking to pick up the two-million-dollar reward. She offered to pay for outside security guards to keep me safe."

"She did?" Zeke leaned in closer, forearms on knees. "Does that mean she doesn't trust everybody on this assignment?"

"It sure looks that way. I'm not sure that she places a lot of faith in Garth's gangland contacts. And she seems to want to be friends with me."

The smell of Zeke's aftershave was hanging faintly in the air between them, an aroma that had now become as familiar as her own perfume. The citrusy scent was comforting and calming, like a warm blanket enveloping her body after she came in from the cold. If she didn't leave this house soon, she was in danger of losing herself in him again. And that was a really bad idea.

"I guess Mrs. Volto's experience of the criminal world makes her suspicious," Zeke said. "She's been surrounded by liars and thieves and cheaters for a long time, and she's smart enough to realize that their information isn't always truthful. But she seems to trust you."

"I don't think she's such a bad person after all," Goldie said. "Her lawyer is shady, but she's only trying to create a good life for her child. I can't fault her for that."

"I certainly don't disagree that Willy Murphy is shady," Zeke said. "And I have no idea what Mrs. Volto sees in him."

"Willy is her safety net." Goldie had a much more acute understanding of why Mrs. Volto was drawn to the powerfulness of her lawyer. "When a person is vulnerable, they look for a protector, someone who'll take care of them and chase away the bad guys. It's hard carrying a burden alone." She closed her eyes. "It's so much easier to share the load with someone who won't crumble under the strain, someone strong and capable."

She opened her eyes, stopping herself from adding, *someone like you*.

Zeke was gazing at her, apparently reading between the lines. "Is that how you feel sometimes?"

"Me? Of course not." She lifted her chin. "I don't need anyone to chase away the bad guys." She made a fist. "I can do that all by myself."

He smiled. "It doesn't hurt to have a little help though, right?"

"Help is fine," she replied. "As long as it doesn't tread on my toes."

He laughed. "Trust me, Goldie, your toes are safe with me."

Zeke watched Goldie as she browsed one of Mrs. Volto's interior design magazines at the kitchen table, slowly and methodically turning the pages while drinking her coffee. She looked so calm and serene that he could almost forget she was the subject of a two-million-dollar bounty hunt. What's more, he could almost imagine that she hadn't built up an impenetrable inner wall, one that shielded her from emotional pain and pushed away all forms of love, even those that would heal her wounds.

Still focusing all her attention on the magazine, she said, "Why are you staring at me?"

He quickly averted his eyes. "I'm not staring. I just thought you hated those magazines, that's all."

She put down her coffee cup. "Come on, Zeke, spit it out."

"Spit what out?"

"Whatever's on your mind."

"I was just thinking," he said, leaning against the kitchen counter, folding his arms. "That someone as beautiful as you would normally think highly of herself. But you don't. You put yourself last all the time, and I don't know why that is."

"I don't put myself last," she argued.

"Yes, you do," he said. "When we have dinner, you always make sure everybody gets served before you, and you're the first one to clear away the dishes. When Angela couldn't sleep because of her headache last night, you gave her your last two painkillers even though I knew you'd need them for your ankle. You put everybody else's needs above your own."

"It's called humility, Zeke," she said with a terse smile. "I guess you wouldn't understand."

He wasn't buying it. "It goes deeper than humility. It's like you don't feel entitled to have good things, or to be special in any way." He walked toward her. "But you *are* special, Goldie, you really are."

"Cut it out," she said sharply. "I don't want to talk about me."

He stopped in his tracks, not wanting to push her further emotionally than she was prepared to go.

"I'm here if you ever want to talk," he said with what he hoped was a supportive tone. "I'm a good listener."

"What I really want from you is the one thing you're not prepared to give," she said. "So your offer to be a good listener is moot."

He realized that Goldie would never appreciate his point of view if he didn't start sharing more personal details with her. He needed her to know why he was so resistant to her request for an apology.

"About three years ago, I was part of a great church," he said. "It was like a family where I was loved and supported."

She looked up at him. "Is this relevant to anything?"

"Something bad happened at that church, which threatened to unsettle the whole dynamic, so I chose to keep the peace. I chose to accept responsibility for something that wasn't my fault, and I've regretted it ever since. If I'd been stronger, I'd still be part of that church and the outcome would've been different for me."

"Are you finished?" She returned her attention to her magazine, slowly turning the pages. "Great story, Zeke."

"I'm trying to tell you that false apologies don't make anything better." He sighed. "You need to understand where I'm coming from."

"I understand where you're coming from," she said. "I just don't agree."

In the background, the front door opened and raised voices echoed through the house, interspersed with a low and mournful cry. Zeke recognized Karl's voice first. And it was furious.

"Go pack your things and be ready to leave

in one hour," he said. "You're officially discharged."

"But sir, it was an emergency." Angela was obviously upset. "I'm so sorry. It won't happen again."

Zeke and Goldie exchanged a glance of confusion and concern before rushing into the hallway to find out exactly what was going on. There in the wide and gleaming foyer were Karl, Garth and Angela. Meanwhile, Mrs. Volto and Willy were making their way upstairs, the lawyer muttering about a lack of professionalism and a likely claim for compensation.

"What happened?" Zeke asked, noticing Angela crying quietly.

Karl was agitated and angry. "Agent Martin disappeared for a whole hour while Mrs. Volto was waiting to take the stand this afternoon. She caused a widespread panic as we searched the entire courthouse for her. We thought she'd been kidnapped, or worse." He refused to look at her as he spoke. "We found her outside in the parking lot on her cell phone." He threw his hands into the air. "On her cell phone!"

"I'm so sorry," Angela said through her tears. "My son is having problems with an addiction, and he needed my help. I was trying to counsel him through a dark moment."

"Your priority is Louisa Volto," Karl shouted. "Whatever personal problems you might be having are not our concern. This is your second lapse in judgment, and we simply cannot tolerate your poor performance any longer." He sagged, as if expended of energy. "You're off the case."

Angela gave a small nod of acceptance and headed for the stairs, wiping her eyes, while Zeke struggled to keep up with yet another surprising turn of events.

"Mrs. Volto needs two protection agents, sir," he said. "Will you be acting as a replacement?"

Karl rubbed at his forehead, sighing. "I wish I could, but it's my job to oversee the entire security detail, both inside and outside the courthouse. I can't dedicate all my time to Mrs. Volto."

"But she's due in court early tomorrow. Do you have time to source somebody else?"

"No," Karl replied. "We're gonna need you to step into Angela's shoes for the time being, Zeke."

"But what about Goldie? She's been coming under attack."

"As far as Agent Phillips and I are concerned, Goldie's situation here is safe and stable, and she can be protected by two police officers while you're gone."

"But…" he began.

"No buts, Zeke." Karl strode past him, punching numbers into his cell phone. "I expect you to follow orders."

Zeke leaned against the wall as Goldie shrugged in resignation. She might not be worried about her safety, but he sure was. He would no longer be there when danger struck. Police officers weren't as highly trained as agents, and they didn't know Goldie like he did.

She might be driving him to distraction, but he still wanted to be by her side. If it didn't sound so crazy, he would say that what he felt for her was a lot like love.

SIX

Standing at the hallway mirror, Zeke straightened his tie and flattened his collar, feeling distinctly uncomfortable in his dark suit on this hot morning. The sun had just risen in a cloudless sky, but he'd been awake for two hours already, unable to sleep for worrying about Goldie's serious situation that day. Who would be protecting her? Would she be safe without him? How could he possibly rid his stomach of this swirling acid anxiety?

"Good morning, Agent Miller." Karl was trotting down the stairs, in his usual navy-blue pants and white shirt. "You're up early. It's great to see that you're so eager to start today's assignment." He placed an earpiece on the table next to the mirror. "You'll need this. We'll be traveling in two cars to the courthouse, and you'll be driving the leading vehicle while Garth drives Mrs. Volto in the one behind. You remember all the security protocols for transporting a high-value witness, right?"

"Of course." Zeke took a deep breath, realizing that Karl was under a lot of stress and unlikely to take kindly to any kind of dissent. Careful words were needed. "I'm still worried about Goldie, sir."

Karl put a hand on Zeke's shoulder. "I've got the best Philadelphia police officers assigned to stay with her until we return from court."

"You do?"

"Absolutely. Officers Brandon Diaz and Leon Moss are two of the most experienced and well-trained officers in the Philly PD. They've worked plenty of classified cases before, so we can trust them implicitly."

"Isn't Officer Diaz the person who got tied up and locked in the garage when Marsha Volto gained access to the house?"

"Yes, he is, but that was hardly his fault. He was ambushed, and Goldie failed to check the credentials of the person standing guard. If she'd only looked at the ID badge, she'd have immediately realized that Marsha Volto was the wrong gender to be Brandon Diaz. He is a good officer with an exemplary record." A knock sounded on the door. "Ah, here they are now. Right on time."

While Karl greeted the uniformed officers with hearty handshakes, Zeke reminded himself that he needed to obey orders and deliver the highest standard of professionalism in order to remain on the case. A car had collected Angela the previous evening and taken her to the train station to make the journey back to Washington, where she would face a disciplinary panel. Zeke didn't want to end up in the same boat.

"Good morning, Officers," he said, smiling and shaking hands. "I want to thank you for stepping in and protecting Agent Simmons today. I'm sure you're already aware of her situation."

"I have to admit that I was amazed when we were told she'd never left Gladwyne," Officer Moss said, removing his hat and jacket to hang them in the closet. "The guys on the force assumed she was a million miles away from here."

"It's a neat little trick," Officer Diaz said with a wry smile. "There's no way that Leonardo Volto would've expected her to hide out in his own wife's house, right under his nose." He laughed. "I gotta say, it's a genius idea."

"It's actually a necessity," Karl said. "Due to the concern about a leak somewhere in the chain of command, we're concerned about moving Agent Simmons to a new safe house. That's why we drafted you two onto the case. You both have a proven record in maintaining secrecy on cases like this, so you're now officially part of a very exclusive club. Only a handful of the most trusted people are aware that Agent Simmons is here, so let's keep it that way."

They answered in unison. "Yes, sir."

"Make yourselves at home," Karl said, striding off down the hallway. "Zeke and Garth can answer any questions you have."

While Officer Moss made his way into the living room, Officer Diaz let out a low whistle, checking out the ornamental mirrors, glittering overhead chandelier and curved staircase. "I guess crime does pay, huh, Agent Miller?"

From the corner of his eye, Zeke saw Goldie emerge into the upstairs hallway, and he quickly steered the wide-eyed officer to the side, speaking quietly.

"I hope you'll take extra care today, Officer Diaz. After what happened with Marsha Volto, I expect you've learned some valuable lessons about security." He glanced up as Goldie descended the stairs. "The subject of your protection assignment is incredibly important to me, and I need to know she's in good hands."

"You can trust me, sir," Officer Diaz said. "I give you my word that I won't let you down."

Zeke smiled. "Thank you. I'll leave my cell phone number on the refrigerator. Call me if you need any advice."

Suddenly, Goldie was behind him, gently moving him aside, holding out a hand to introduce herself.

"Is Agent Miller subjecting you to an old-fashioned shakedown, officer?" she said with a smile. "Whatever he's told you, don't worry. We're perfectly safe here."

Zeke gritted his teeth but said nothing. Why did she have to play down the danger like this?

"I'll do my best to minimize any risks, ma'am," Officer Diaz said. "I'll go take an immediate tour of the house and familiarize myself with the exits. I like to be well-prepared."

As soon as they were alone, Goldie tilted her head to the side and raised her eyebrows, apparently asking a silent question.

"What?" Zeke said with an exaggerated shrug. "I was simply making sure Officer Diaz understood the severity of the situation."

"You were checking up on him," she challenged. "Because you don't trust him."

He couldn't deny this accusation. "I don't trust anyone, Goldie. Except you."

She pursed her lips. "And I thought I was meant to be the one with problems. You're surrounded by great colleagues, and they've got your back. You have to learn to rely on them."

"When it comes to your safety, I'd rather be in control."

She gave him a gentle push back. "Get over yourself, Zeke. You're not my knight in shining armor. I'm a trained agent just like you are."

"Yeah, I know." He rubbed the back of his neck, worried about bringing up this difficult topic again. "But I get the feeling that I'd be more careful with your life than you are."

She rolled her eyes. "Not this again. I'm trying really hard to build up my self-worth. It's not easy, but I'm working on it."

He was pleased to hear that. It was a good start. "Did you get around to reading that Bible I left in your room?" he asked, wondering if this might have anything to do with it.

"No."

"Why not?"

"Because I've opened Bibles a hundred

times before," she said. "I've spent hours reading passages and parables that are meant to be meaningful and profound, but they're just stories that don't mean anything to me anymore."

That made him so sad. "You don't find meaning in any of them?"

"No."

Zeke thought of the many passages of scripture that had supported and strengthened him during difficult days—those that encouraged him to cast his anxieties onto God and to trust in a wisdom that surpassed all understanding. He couldn't imagine facing life without these vital sources of comfort and wished that Goldie could see things the same way.

"Maybe it would help if I wrote some verses down for you," he suggested. "You might not be finding the most inspirational ones."

She shook her head. "No, thank you. I'm fine."

He grabbed a pen and notepad from the hallway table. "Are you sure? It won't take a second."

"Let it drop, Zeke."

He placed the pen and pad back on the table. "I wish you'd let me in a little more," he said, deciding that a gentler approach might work better. "And stop being determined to be mad at me."

"I need to be mad at someone," she said, folding her arms protectively. "Otherwise I have to accept that God hates me."

His mouth dropped open. "How on earth could you reach that conclusion?"

"Think about all the things that happened to pull us apart." She began to check the events off on her fingers. "My dad forced us to leave town in the middle of the night. Your dad destroyed my letters. Your parents changed their phone number so I couldn't call. You moved away from Glenside only a few weeks before I managed to get to your house." She let out a groan of frustration. "Are things really that random? Or was somebody out to destroy our relationship?"

He could see what she was getting at. "You're asking me if God is to blame?"

"Well, if neither of us is at fault, then He's the only one left to take the blame." She stared down at her feet. "And if He deliberately crushed our love, then I guess it means He doesn't much care for me."

"God doesn't set out to cause us pain," Zeke said. "He only wants what's best for us."

"So why did He make me so miserable by letting us lose each other?"

He sighed. Goldie sure knew how to wallow in misery. "Life is like a series of chapters. When you're in the middle of the book, you don't know how it'll end. You have no idea how our story would've played out if we'd stayed in Glenside and settled down like we'd planned. Anything could've happened. We might've split up because we were too young and immature. You'd most likely never have joined the army or the Bureau, and you wouldn't be the person you are today."

"I don't know, Zeke," she said with a look of skepticism. "It all sounds a little too convenient for my liking, like using the excuse that God's always in control. Why can't you just tell me that God messed up and let me be mad at Him?"

"Because God didn't mess up and blaming Him isn't helping you."

She fell silent, but he saw her fists clench at her sides, her knuckles white. "I guess if God didn't mess up then it has to be on you."

"You're your own worst enemy, Goldie," he said, letting his impatience get the better of him. "I don't think you really want to grow and change. You just want to punish the world for hurting you. Or punish me at least."

"Is that what you think I'm trying to do?" she asked. "You think I'm trying to punish you?"

"Well, aren't you?"

"No." She sounded genuinely pained. "I'm trying to make sense of what happened, to learn to accept that everything I had planned out in my life came to nothing." She threw her hands in the air. "What was the point in all those years we spent growing up together, falling in love, learning about each other, mapping our future? It was simply wasted time. I feel like I've been robbed, so please don't tell me not to be angry. I don't know how to be anything else right now."

"All I'm asking is that you try to stop hurting me because of the past," he said. "We've already established that I don't think there's anything more I could've done."

"Yes," she said firmly. "I understand that perfectly."

"I don't know what I can do to help you, Goldie," he said with exasperation. "I've tried everything and you only push me away."

"Everything?" she challenged. "You think you've tried everything?"

"Yes." He knew where she was leading him. "Almost everything."

"Everything apart from apologizing, right?"

Zeke felt that Goldie was driving him to the brink of madness. "I really do care about you, Goldie, far more than you realize, but we're continually going around in circles. If only you'd listen to me when I try to give you advice, you might be able to move forward, but you're always putting up barriers, finding reasons to pin your unhappiness on everybody else's shoulders but yours."

She blinked as if he had slapped her. "If that's how you feel, then I guess this conversation is done."

He wondered if perhaps he had gone too far. "I really do want to help you, but sometimes I get frustrated."

"Help me?" she queried. "Like some sort of charity case."

"No, not like a charity case." He really was making a mess of this. "Like a friend."

"We're not friends, Zeke," she said. "I don't know what we are to each other now, but we're certainly not friends."

That comment stung. "I thought we were doing okay," he said. "Why can't we be friends?"

She rolled her eyes. "You're always telling me what to do, when to pray, what to feel, how to be a better person. It's like I'm your little project or something."

He was taken aback and more than a little hurt by that. "I don't see you as a project."

"Yes, you do. You're trying to mold me into being somebody else, somebody better."

"I'm not. I'm just trying to help."

"I don't need your help, because I'm fine with being a hot mess." Pivoting on the ball of one foot, she swiveled away from him melodramatically. "Thanks for the chat, Zeke. It was superhelpful."

She stalked in the direction of the kitchen, and Zeke squeezed his forehead with an index finger and thumb. Goldie really infuriated him with her closed-mindedness and determination to hold on to hurt. She seemed like a lost cause, and he sometimes wondered whether to give up on her. Was the heartache really worth it?

"I won't give up on her just yet," he muttered under his breath, rallying himself. "Let's give it just one more day."

Goldie opened the fridge and took a deep lungful of cool, crisp air, letting the white vapor glide over the layer of sweat on her face.

"I can't believe that the air-conditioning chose today of all days to stop working," she said. "It must be more than one hundred degrees outside."

"One hundred and three to be exact, ma'am," Officer Diaz said. "Extreme heat warnings have been issued by the local forecasters."

Goldie closed the refrigerator door and picked up her damp cloth from the kitchen counter. As soon as she pressed it to her forehead, it became apparent that the ice she had placed inside the folds just ten minutes ago had melted away, and the fabric was now tepid and unwelcome on her skin.

"Oh, this is ridiculous," she said, tossing the cloth aside. "Did you call the technician?"

"Yes, ma'am," Officer Diaz replied. "But the sudden heat has caused a lot of technical problems today, and I've been told that a technician might take a few hours to arrive."

She slid down the side of the wall and sat with her legs outstretched, hands flat on the tiled floor, desperately trying to glean some coolness from the ceramic. But, like everything else, the tiles were warm and clammy.

"The whole house feels like it's sweating," she said. "It's excruciating."

"It would certainly help if we could open the drapes and windows on the shady side of the house," Officer Moss said, fanning himself with a magazine. "But that's strictly against the rules."

Goldie wiped her brow with the back of her hand and jutted her bottom lip to try to blow some damp tendrils from her face. With the house constantly shrouded in darkness and lit by artificial light, she imagined that the bulbs themselves were emitting a scorching heat to mingle with the awful humidity that pervaded every corner of every room. Wearing shorts and a tank top didn't help in the slightest. She wanted to be immersed in water.

"I think I'm gonna melt into a puddle right here on the floor," she said. "Would you guys think I'm totally crazy if I said I wanted to take a swim in the pool?"

Officer Moss laughed. "Taking a swim wouldn't make you crazy, but it might get us fired. We're not supposed to let you go outside."

She stood up, her bare feet slightly swollen, skin stretched tight. "Actually, I can do what I choose. You're here to oversee my protection, but not to decide my movements. I'm still an agent of the FBI, and I get to weigh the risks."

Officer Diaz took a sip of water from a glass on the kitchen counter. Both officers had removed their ties and rolled up their shirtsleeves, but Officer Diaz had also taken off his shoes and folded up the hems of his pants. The overall effect meant that he looked a little like a ship's castaway, and he sat on a stool at the breakfast bar, wiping his neck with a cloth.

"Technically, ma'am," he said, "you out-rank us, so we take orders from you, not the other way around."

She smiled. "That's what I thought." She closed her eyes for a few seconds to imagine slipping into the beautiful chill of water. It would envelop her, saturate her hot scalp and soothe her swollen feet. "The drone jamming technology is installed now, right?"

"Yes, ma'am," Officer Moss replied. "Any drone that tries to fly within two miles of this house will be neutralized."

"That means nothing with a signal can fly into the yard and hurt me." She walked to the kitchen window and teased the blind aside. There was the pool, glinting in the haze, a muggy breeze sending small waves lapping across the surface. "What about a sniper?"

Officer Moss appeared behind her and peeked through the small gap she'd created in the blind. "The security fence is too high for a shooter to hit you from close by." He pointed to the rolling countryside beyond, the kind of view that only the very wealthy could afford in the suburbs. "A sniper would have to be way up in those hills to stand a chance of getting a direct line of sight."

"So he'd have to be a professional marksman?"

"Yes, ma'am. I'd say he'd only be able to take a shot from a mile away. And there's the humidity to think of too. I'm no expert sniper, but these conditions would make it very difficult for a bullet to find its target."

She continued to stare at the pool, taking a big, deep breath and letting it out slowly. "That means I'm probably perfectly safe to take a quick dip."

"On balance of probabilities, you'd be fine," Officer Moss replied. "But there's a price of two million dollars on your head, so please don't even consider taking the risk."

As a bead of sweat snaked its way down her back, she couldn't help but contemplate it.

Officer Diaz slid from his stool at the counter. "I'll stand guard while you swim if you really want to."

"Maybe I should call Agent Miller," Officer Moss said. "And run it by him first."

As if Zeke had a hotline to the conversation in the room, Goldie's cell began to buzz across the counter, his name on the display. She picked it up and hit the answer button.

"Are you checking up on me?" she asked.

"Yes." There was a low hum of voices in the background. "The court is on a break, so I checked in with Karl at the office. He tells me that your AC is broken and he's struggling to get a repairman to you. How are you holding up in this heat?"

"It's like being inside a metal box that's buried in a firepit," she said. "It's unbearable."

"That sucks, but you'll have to bear it because there's no other option."

She fell silent.

"Goldie," he said slowly. "You're not thinking of doing something stupid, are you?"

"No," she lied. "Absolutely not."

"Good. Because I'm certain that a bounty hunter knows you're at the house, and if you go outside, he'll target you. And you'll place everybody in danger."

"I know," she said with a sigh. "That's why I'm staying indoors."

"Promise me," he said with a tone of condescension. "I need to hear you promise."

"Stop patronizing me, Zeke. And stop calling."

"Wait, Goldie—"

She hung up the phone and tossed it

roughly back on the counter. Then she re-wetted her cloth and held it to her temple.

"My conscience just called," she said. "I guess we'll be staying in the sweatbox after all."

"Goldie?" Zeke continued to hold the phone to his ear. "Are you there?" He moved the cell away from his head and stared at it. "She hung up on me."

Garth patted him on the shoulder as they both stood outside the door that led to the judge's chambers. Mrs. Volto had broken down in tears numerous times while giving evidence that morning, so the trial judge had ordered a short recess to give her time to compose herself, allowing her the use of his own private space to do so. At that moment, Willy was giving his client a pep talk, likely reminding her that her husband had no power to hurt her in a packed courtroom dotted with armed guards.

"Are you surprised she hung up on you?" Garth asked. "You're checking up on her like she's a child. Goldie is a grown woman who can take responsibility for herself. Give her some space."

Zeke was surprised at the rebuke. "You think I patronize her?"

"A little." As he spoke, Garth's roving eye

scanned the corridor, across the people wandering through. "I know you two have history, and it's none of my business, but sometimes when you talk to her you seem kinda…" He stopped, clearly uncertain which word should follow. "Smug."

Now Zeke was even more surprised. "Smug?"

"Yeah, like you have all the answers and she's just a screwup."

Zeke's mouth dropped open. In all of his dealings with Goldie, he never once considered himself condescending or arrogant. But maybe he was wrong.

"I don't think Goldie's a screwup," he said.

Garth side-eyed him, one eyebrow sliding upward. "You don't?"

"Not really." He considered all of Goldie's flaws. "I think she makes bad choices, even when alarm bells should be ringing. She's stubborn and won't listen to reason. She's argumentative. She holds on to grudges and past hurts. And she drives me to distraction because she can't see how amazing she truly is."

"Wow." Garth sucked air through his teeth. "I had no idea you were this crazy in love with her."

"What? That's stupid. We were over a long

time ago. I'm just a friend trying to help her figure some stuff out."

"Okay, if you say so."

"It's true," he said, knowing that his protestations would make him sound as though he had something to hide. "I want her to be happy."

"I'm guessing you also want her to think like you do, right? And believe in the same things?"

"Well, sorta," he said. "I can see where she's going wrong, and I think I can help her."

Garth shook his head, a hint of a smile on his face. "See, that's what I'm talking about, man," he said. "Smug."

Zeke stared down at his shoes, replaying the conversations he'd had with Goldie over these last few days, remembering her accusation that he sat on a high horse. Had he shut her down without realizing? Had he judged her as a screwup and assumed he knew all the answers? Garth's insight was enlightening.

He placed a hand on his colleague's shoulder. "If someone wanted to stop behaving like a smug idiot, how would you suggest he goes about it?" He smiled sheepishly. "I'm asking for a friend."

Garth laughed. "I'd advise *your friend* not to criticize or get mad when she's trying to explain how she feels. Try to see things from her point of view. She's got a tough exterior but it's clearly an act. Inside she's scared and hurting and all she really wants is for someone to hold her and tell her everything will be fine. People in pain will lash out because they don't know how to ask for affection."

This made perfect sense. Goldie had lashed out numerous times since they'd reconnected, but Zeke had naturally assumed it was because she was angry with him. Could she really just be desperately waiting for him to hug her and hold her tight?

"How do you know this kind of stuff?" he asked. "You sound like quite an expert."

"The Bureau sent me on a psychology course a few years back," Garth replied. "It taught me a lot about the human condition. We only need food and water to survive, but we need love to thrive. People can eventually die without love."

"I don't doubt it," Zeke said, wondering who filled this particular hole in Goldie's life. He had a family who made a fuss over him, bought him thoughtful gifts and sent sweet messages inside birthday cards. But he also had access to a greater source of love than even his family. He had God, and he wanted Goldie to feel His presence in her life too.

"If you really want what's best for Goldie," Garth said, "let her walk at her own pace."

Zeke took the words to heart. "I had no clue you were such a fount of wisdom," he said with admiration.

Garth nodded a greeting as a woman in a red dress walked past, smiling coyly at them. "Yeah, the ladies assume I'm nothing but beefcake, but these waters run deep."

Zeke burst into laughter while Garth remained deadpan, playing up the serious side of his character.

"Thanks for the advice," Zeke said, using his thumbs to wipe moisture from beneath his eyes. "It helped a lot."

"That's good. I'm glad to be of assistance."

The door behind them opened and Willy walked into the corridor, closely followed by Mrs. Volto, whose mascara was streaked beneath her eyes. Willy stopped and waited for his client to reach his side, whereupon he slid his arm around her shoulder protectively.

"Our recess is almost at an end." The case judge came striding along the corridor, his robe swishing through the air. "Mr. Murphy, is Mrs. Volto ready to reconvene?"

Willy gave a swift nod. "We're ready, Judge Barton."

The judge clapped his hands and rubbed

them together. "Excellent." Turning to Zeke, he said, "Agent Miller, would you like to lead the way?"

"Yes, sir."

The judge smiled. "Let's get this session wrapped up as soon as possible. It's the hottest day of the year out there, and I have a pool waiting for me at home."

Zeke's chest gave an involuntary flutter as he started off down the corridor. With no air-conditioning in Mrs. Volto's house and all the windows closed, the pool must seem incredibly inviting. But Goldie was smarter than that. She may be reckless but leaving the safety of the house in broad daylight was a step too far, even for her.

Wasn't it?

Goldie paced in the kitchen, pressing the cloth to her nape and shoulders, groaning in the heat. The officers were performing a routine patrol, walking the outside perimeter, leaving her locked inside. She felt sorry for them, forced out into the searing heat, wearing full uniform. At least she could wear shorts and a tank top.

She teased aside the blind, taking another look at the pool in the hope that its shimmering coolness might just be enough to drop her body temperature a little.

In the next moment, she leaped back from the window, a hand flying to her mouth. In the pool was a person, facedown on the surface, wearing what looked like a police uniform, a peaked cap floating nearby.

"No!" she shouted, reaching for her cell phone on the counter. "This can't be happening."

She rushed as quickly as she could to the patio door, limping on her painful ankle while frantically searching for Karl's number in her contacts.

"Karl!" she yelled when he answered. "Get an ambulance here now. One of the officers is drowning."

"What? Who? How?"

She unlocked the door and opened it wide, the heat of the day hitting her like a sauna. "I don't know who or how, but I have to go drag him out."

The reply was swift and loud. "No! His colleague can help him. You have to stay inside."

But she was already running out onto the baking tiles, flitting in bare feet, ignoring the discomfort in her injured foot.

"There's nobody else around," she said,

sweat beads already snaking down her brow. "Only I can help him right now."

"Goldie." Karl was speaking slowly and deliberately. "I'm ordering you to remain inside. Help is on the way."

As she neared the pool, she could see the man more clearly, definitely wearing the jacket of a police officer.

"He's drowning, sir. And I won't stand by and watch it happen."

She tossed the cell aside, raced toward the water and used her good foot to launch herself into the pool. She dived headfirst, the coolness of the water folding around her, exquisite on her skin.

Yet there was no time to enjoy the sensation because the floating man needed her help. She reached out to take hold of him, grabbing his jacket and yanking it toward her. The figure was light and easily moved as it rolled over in the water. That's when she realized that the form was simply a torso. No arms, no legs, no head.

"What is this?" she said to herself in confusion, pulling at the jacket, tugging it open to reveal a smooth fabric interior. "Is this a dummy?"

She gasped in horror, acknowledging she had been duped. This wasn't a police officer. It was a dressmaker's dummy.

"Oh no." She scrambled for the side. "I gotta get out of here."

The first bullet slammed into the dummy, splitting the chest wide open to allow the foam innards to spill out. Goldie now had no time to reach the side. She had to go under.

"Stay out of sight," she yelled to the officers, as she saw them run along the path that led from the front of the house. "There's a sniper."

Taking a huge gulp of air, she dived to the bottom of the pool, where she sat cross-legged on the tiles, her mind racing with possibilities, trying to come up with an escape strategy. There had to be a way out of this. There had to be.

But multiple streaks were entering the water, creating what looked like small airplane vapor trails. They traveled around four or five feet into the water before slowing to a halt. Then she saw the bullets slowly drift and sink, before hearing them make a distinct and chilling clink on the fiberglass bottom.

Her chest tight, she desperately wanted to inhale, but clamped a hand across her mouth and concentrated on staying alert. The bullets continued to snake through the water, tiny missiles seeking her out, but their penetration was limited to around five feet. If she remained deeper than that, she would be safe. Squeezing her eyes shut, she silently spoke to God.

Please, she begged. *I know I don't deserve Your mercy, but don't let my life end this way.*

She sat dead still, opening her eyes to watch the bullets enter the pool, high speed at first, their energy being slowly absorbed by the density of the water. In any other setting, the scene might even be described as beautiful, the tiny pockets of air dancing and popping before her. Yet these mesmerizing trails were deadly, just one of them able to rip her flesh apart.

Bright stars swirled before her eyes. She needed to breathe. The constriction in her chest was agonizing, and her entire body cried out for air. She had to take a chance. Making her way to the surface, she reached up with her hands, ready to break through, but a pain in her bicep threw her off guard and off trajectory. Rolling in the water, she was aware of thin ribbons of blood twirling around her. A bullet had grazed her skin, creating an angry red laceration.

Her head was growing dizzier by the second, making her limbs heavy and her vision blurred. As Zeke's face settled in her mind, she became aware that she was falling, cushioned by the water, descending to a watery grave.

SEVEN

Zeke watched Mrs. Volto answer questions on the stand, a tissue in one hand and a glass of water in the other. Occasionally, she would pause for breath or to take a sip of water before continuing her testimony. Zeke had to admit that she was an incredibly convincing and sympathetic witness, the straining fabric across her baby bump lending her a distinct vulnerability. She had also been careful to wear little makeup and style her hair modestly, lest the jurors judge her as a privileged and extravagant wife of a gangster. Willy had advised his client with a shrewd and clever eye for detail, and he had a front row seat to watch the action unfold, as the two opposing counsels slugged it out in the courtroom.

"Is it true, Mrs. Volto," the prosecutor said, walking toward the stand, "that you were placed under immense pressure by your husband to keep his crimes secret from the authorities?"

She dabbed the tissue on her nose and sniffed. "Yes."

"Did Mr. Volto ever use violence against you to ensure your compliance?"

"Yes."

"Can you elaborate, please?" The prosecutor touched the wooden surround of the witness box. "I understand that this subject is a painful business, but please try to tell us in your own words exactly what forms of abuse you suffered at the hands of Leonardo Volto."

From his position standing at the side of the court, Zeke glanced at Mr. Volto, whose face was scarlet with apparent fury, fists clenched on the table in front of him. His lawyer leaned across and whispered in his ear, most likely warning his client against showing any form of aggression. It was not a good look to a jury.

"Leonardo would often slap me or pull my hair or punch my stomach." She placed a hand on her bump and rubbed. "That's why I have to do everything possible to save this little one from being hurt. Leo said that if I ever betrayed him, he would cut me into a thousand pieces and mail them to my father, even while I'm carrying his child."

Audible gasps could be heard around the

room, this revelation shocking even the hardiest of courtroom personnel. But Zeke was more surprised than most, because Mrs. Volto had steadfastly maintained that her husband would never hurt their baby. She had either lied previously or she was lying now.

"Thank you, Mrs. Volto," the prosecutor said, retaking his seat, deciding to end on this bombshell. "I have no further questions."

Mr. Volto's defense attorney leaped to his feet. "Mrs. Volto," he began, making his way out from behind the counsel table. "I'm a little confused."

Mrs. Volto raised her eyebrows. "That can happen sometimes as we get older."

Laughter fluttered through the court and the attorney smiled defensively, waiting for the snickering to die away.

"Mr. Volto has wanted to become a father for a good many years, and his dream has finally come true." He gestured toward his client. "Now why on earth would Mr. Volto want to cut you into a thousand pieces if it would harm his precious baby?"

Mrs. Volto said nothing.

"He is either an abusive and wicked man, or he is a doting father," the attorney said. "Which is it?"

"He is an abuser," she said defiantly.

The defense counsel returned to his desk to read some notes, taking his time.

"I don't think your baby is in any danger at all, Mrs. Volto," he said dramatically. "I think your main concern is finding a way to hold on to the money that your successful husband has amassed through his business dealings, not to mention the mansion with its gated drive and private pool."

At the mention of the pool, Zeke was reminded of his earlier fear about how far Goldie was prepared to go in order to escape the unbearable heat, and he steadied himself against the wall, a sudden and unwelcome sense of dread sinking into his belly. Danger seemed to be closing around him, and his body automatically went on high alert, scanning the room for signs of threat. He found none. This threat clearly wasn't in his vicinity.

"I need my house and money to enable me to provide for my child," Mrs. Volto said, wiping her streaky eyes. "I'm doing this for my baby."

The attorney smiled slyly. "Oh, please spare us the false emotion, Mrs. Volto. You turned on your husband because of your own selfish greed. And if you're prepared to lie in court about my client's alleged abusive behavior, what else are you lying about?"

Zeke didn't hear the answer because he suddenly became preoccupied with Goldie's safety. He knew that she was hotheaded and stubborn. What if she had ignored his advice about remaining inside? What if the dire heat had forced her to seek respite in the pool? But she wouldn't do that, would she?

Yes, she would.

Signaling a comfort break to Garth, who was overseeing proceedings on the opposite side of the courtroom, Zeke pulled out his cell phone and rushed into the corridor.

His heart was telling him that Goldie needed an answer to a prayer.

Goldie felt herself being tugged and jolted, her body as limp as a rag doll. She was on the verge of opening her mouth and inhaling water, but someone was pulling her toward the surface, holding her face upward, telling her to breathe.

She coughed and spluttered, urgently gasping for lifesaving air, while Officer Moss guided her to the edge of the pool. With a huge groan, he pushed her onto the warm tiles, where she lay like a wet fish, exhausted, in the shadow of a black wall on wheels.

She pointed at it. "What is this?"

"It's a portable ballistic shield, and it's entirely bulletproof," Officer Moss said, hauling himself out of the water to crouch next to her. "I got it from the panic room."

"How did you know it was there?"

"I got a call from Agent Miller while I panicked about how I could get out here and help you. I explained that you were trapped in the pool, and he told me exactly what to do." He raised his eyes skyward. "It's a good thing he called, because that sniper isn't going away any time soon and the backup officers can't get into the yard without coming under attack."

As if to prove his point, bullets pinged off the black metal, and Goldie shifted herself closer to the safety of the panel, which was just wide enough to cover them both. She waited for a lull in the fire before speaking again.

"Where's Diaz?"

"He put on a bulletproof vest and jumped the barbed wire fence to go look for the shooter. I hope he's okay. I told him not to go, but he said he wanted to take him down before you got hurt."

Goldie checked her wound, saw blood mingling with the water on her skin to trickle down her arm and onto her hand. Despite the intense heat, her body was shivering, and she desperately wanted Zeke there with her. His safe arms were suddenly all she could think of.

"Let's go." Officer Moss stood in a hunched posture and positioned himself flat against the panel, holding on to a handle in the center. "All we need to do is stay behind this shield while we wheel it back to the house. Slow and steady. Can you do that? Is your ankle strong enough?"

Still with Zeke's face in her mind, Goldie forced her shaking legs to stand. She had found some inner strength.

"Right at this moment," she said, "I can do anything."

Zeke rushed into the house, calling Goldie's name. Since his phone call with Officer Moss earlier that day, he had been unable to think of anyone other than her. Karl had updated him on the situation during a court break, letting him know that Goldie was safe, but the hours had dragged into infinity, right up until the moment the jury retired for the day.

"I'm here, I'm fine." Goldie was standing at the top of the stairs, wearing shorts and a T-shirt, a white bandage wound around her arm. "I just got a little graze from a bullet."

Karl appeared in the hallway, cheeks flushed with either stress or heat. Or both.

"The central air unit has been tampered with," he said. "A technician is outside right now, working on the broken unit."

"Who did it?" Zeke asked. "And why?"

"I can only assume that the intention was to force Goldie outside to escape the heat inside," he replied. "And when that didn't work, a tailor's dummy from the garage was thrown into the pool wearing a police jacket to make it appear as though one of the officers was facedown in the water."

"How could somebody get hold of a police uniform?"

"It's a fake one, like a party costume, but from a distance it looks just like the real thing."

Zeke took off his jacket and loosened his tie. "One of the officers is certain to be the culprit," he said. "Only they would've known the perfect opportunity to strike. Where are they now?"

"They're being interviewed at headquarters, but I have to say that they both appeared to do a stand-up job today. They saved Goldie's life. Officer Moss got her back into the house while Officer Diaz apprehended the shooter."

"Then what on earth happened here today, sir?" Zeke said. "Who is doing these things?"

"That's what we need to discuss," Karl said. "We're having a crisis meeting in the cinema room in two hours. It's the coolest room in the house, but that's not saying much, so I suggest you change into something a little less formal."

Zeke looked down at his black suit pants. "I'll be ready."

He started up the stairs, leaving his jacket on the banister and removing his tie.

As he neared the top, Goldie held up a palm, like a traffic cop signaling a stop. "I know what you're gonna say, Zeke, so I'll save you the trouble. I should never have gone outside. I was stupid not to realize it was a trap, and I should be more careful next time." She folded her arms. "Does that just about sum it up?"

She looked beyond his shoulder, at a fixed point on the wall, unwilling to meet his gaze. Her skin was pale, but dark circles had formed beneath her eyes and she was clenching her jaw, possibly holding back tears. She was forlorn, most likely embarrassed at having been fooled once again, and not likely to respond well to criticism. Remembering his conversation with Garth, Zeke took a step forward and gathered her into his arms, cradling the back of her head, feeling the heat of her nape on his cupped hand.

"Everything will be fine, Goldie," he whispered. "I promise."

The stiffness in her body loosened in an instant, each of her limbs relaxing and leaning into him. Then she slid her arms around his waist and rested her cheek on his shoulder, sighing sadly.

"I wasn't expecting this reaction from you," she said quietly. "I thought you'd be mad."

"Why would I be mad?" he asked. "You thought an officer was drowning. And you wanted to risk your life to help him."

She let out a tiny sob, but quickly silenced it. "I thought I was going to drown, right there in that pool, and all I could think about was you."

His heart exploded in a flutter of beats. What exactly was she saying?

"Something is happening between us, isn't it?" he said. "Even though we promised to be strictly professional."

"I can't help it, Zeke. I tried to fight it, but it's not easy pushing you away all the time." She sagged a little more. "It's exhausting."

He allowed himself to enjoy the sensation

of her body in his arms, in spite of the overwhelming heat and humidity.

"I think we both knew that there was a strong chemistry between us," he said. "But we didn't want to acknowledge it. Seeing you again was like slipping back into a familiar routine. I know we argue, but the love is still there, right?"

"I don't know what it is," she said. "But it keeps drawing me toward you and I don't know how to make it go away."

"Do you want to make it go away?" he asked.

"Of course, I do. There's no way you and I can be romantic again, so what's the point in having these feelings if I can't do anything with them?"

He waited a little while before asking his next question, almost certain that he knew the answer but hoping he was wrong anyway.

"Why can't we be romantic again?"

She laughed, not unkindly but loudly enough to let him know that she was dead set against the idea.

"You've got to be kidding me, right? We can barely make it an hour without fighting about the past. You're always trying to force me to change, and I don't think you really listen to me when I talk. You only hear what you want to hear."

"I haven't been much help to you, have I?" he said, looking into her eyes. "I thought I could just drop a Bible on your bed and expect God to do all the hard work for me, but that's not how it works. I know God puts in the hours for us, but I think He expected a little more humility from me. And a little more effort."

"What kind of effort are you talking about?" she asked. "The kind of effort that involves an apology perhaps?"

He ran his gaze across her face, contemplating her words. Could he give her the apology she craved and move forward? If this was the only barrier preventing them from being closer, it was easily removed by the words *I'm sorry.* He willed himself to say them, to be the bigger person and give her the closure that her father had refused to give her. Yet the apology stuck in his throat, suspended there by the memories of how much damage had been done by his past failure to stand his ground. His false apology to Susan had upended his life, driven him from the church, from his friends and his support network. Starting over in a new place of worship had been tough, and he still resented the fact he'd been forced to do it.

"I can't," he said finally. "It may seem like such a simple thing to you, Goldie, but I can't give you an apology when it doesn't come from the heart. It would make me bitter and might even eat away at me." He cupped her face in his hands. "I want to give you everything you need to be happy, but I have to draw a line here, because it would probably destroy us in the end."

"Won't you at least consider whether you could've done things differently?" she asked. "I feel like you've dismissed my pain as collateral damage."

"No," he protested. "How could you think that?"

"You wanted to get on with your life and forget me, so you moved away from the only place I would come looking for you. You took care of your own well-being first and foremost and, even though you didn't mean to hurt me, you ended up breaking my heart." She slid his hands from her face. "I can't think of any other way to describe it than collateral damage. My pain is an unintended consequence of you running away to start over."

Zeke's shirt had begun sticking to his skin,

and his physical discomfort only added to his emotional distress. He felt as though he was stuck in a loop, rehashing the same old problems and feelings, never reaching a conclusion or resolution, but destined to remain in the same place forevermore.

"You already know how I feel about this, Goldie," he said. "I can't bear to see you hurting, but I can't do anything to change it."

She stepped back. "Of course you can. You can own it."

He lifted his eyes to the ceiling, again considering whether this was a blow he could possibly absorb. Not only would an apology help Goldie heal, but it would smooth the way toward a rekindling of their love. They had never gotten over each other, that much was clear, and no woman had ever come close to filling her shoes.

"Your father owns all the hurt that's been inflicted on you," he said. "You know he does. Your issue is with him, not me."

"Does that really matter?" she said. "I just want someone to say *I'm sorry*." Tears were filling her eyes. "Why can't that person be you?"

Closing his eyes briefly, he reminded himself of the damage he could inflict by compromising his principles. "I'm sorry," he said. "I can't."

"I understand," she said, turning to head in the direction of her bedroom. "It's obviously not meant to be."

He watched her disappear into her room, firmly closing the door behind her, as if closing the door on their relationship. He wanted to go after her, to promise her everything she wanted. But how long would he be able to hold out before acrimony set in? How long would it take for their happiness to deteriorate into a quagmire of squabbles and recriminations?

When it came to taking the blame for Goldie's pain, his heart told him yes, but he was determined that this time his head would rule the day.

"Well, here we all are once again," Christina said, standing in front of the huge screen in the cinema room, in an uncharacteristic loose and flowing dress. "I apologize for my informal attire today but it's as hot as the desert out there, so I ditched the suit." She looked around the room at Zeke, Goldie, Garth and Karl, noting the assortment of shorts and T shirts. "And I can see that you guys wisely did the same."

"The technician completed the repair and has left the house," Karl said. "But he said it might take a good hour or so for the central air to start functioning on full capacity."

"It can't come a moment too soon," Christina said, turning to the screen and activating it with the remote control in her hand. An image of the backyard flickered to life, taken from the CCTV camera that was rigged up on the back wall of the house. "I thought I'd show you what happened today and give you an overview of developments."

She pressed the controller in her hand, and the image came to life. Goldie was shamefaced to see herself appear on the screen, flitting across the tile with a slight limp and diving headfirst into the pool to try to save a tailor's dummy.

The screen showed Goldie turning over the dummy, realizing her mistake and staring around the yard in confusion and panic. Then, somewhere in the corner of the yard a light flashed twice, just for a fraction of a second, but bright enough to catch everybody's attention.

Christina paused the image. "There." She pointed to a spot on the top of the fence. "Did you see that? Something flashed right there."

"What was it?" Zeke asked.

Christina held up a cell phone. "It was this phone. It had been stuck into the barbed wire, facing the hills, and was subsequently remotely activated to flash twice."

"It was a signal," Zeke said. "A signal that Goldie was out in the open."

"Correct," Christina replied. "We think that someone was giving the green light to a sniper, letting him know that his target was available. It works on a simple phone signal and can be activated with a touch of a button on another cell. But it requires a close proximity, so the person would have to have been nearby."

"Can't we just check the CCTV footage to see who placed the cell phone there?" Zeke asked. "That should also tell us who pushed the dummy into the pool."

Christina smiled wryly. "Just after 7:00 a.m. this morning, someone obscured the camera lens with this." She picked up a piece of cardboard from a chair next to her and held it aloft. "It was presumably intended to remain there for the entire day but ended up being dislodged when Goldie opened the patio door. Therefore, we have no footage of the culprit or culprits."

"Officers Moss and Diaz are the first people I'd want to question," Zeke said. "They had the time to tamper with the air-conditioning and the CCTV and the opportunity to go into the garage to find a dummy to use as a decoy. It has to be one of them."

Christina nodded. "I agree, but they did such a great job today that I'm not sure I can put them on the list of suspects." She restarted the footage, using the remote to fast-forward. "Here you can see Officer Diaz hauling himself over the barbed wire to try to locate the shooter in the hills. He wisely strapped on a bulletproof vest from his patrol car beforehand." She fast-forwarded again. "And here you can see Officer Moss shielding Goldie with the portable ballistics shield from the panic room, which I have to say was an excellent idea and I'll be putting him forward for a commendation."

Goldie held up a hand. "Actually, that was Zeke's idea, ma'am."

Zeke silenced her with a quick shake of the head.

"What?" she argued. "It *was* your idea."

"Officer Diaz left the scene," Garth said incredulously. "How does that make him a hero?"

"As I already explained, Diaz went in search of the shooter, hoping to root him out at the source. The SWAT team we sent to scour the hills discovered that Diaz had already captured the sniper a few minutes previously. So we have our bad guy in custody thanks to Officer Diaz's quick thinking and bravery. And Goldie is alive thanks to Officer Moss's ingenuity." Christina smiled. "Although it looks like he might've had a helping hand from Agent Miller. Well done, Zeke. Using the ballistics shield was a great idea."

"Who's the shooter?" Goldie asked, wondering if she really wanted to know the name of the person who wanted her dead.

"His name is Marty Foster and he's a former staff sergeant in the Marine Corps. He was something of a legend in the military because of his sharpshooting ability, but he built up quite a poor disciplinary record toward the end of his career. He was bitter about not rising further up the ranks and accused his superiors of jealousy. He was eventually discharged and subsequently served time for armed robbery."

"He sounds like a piece of work," Zeke said, reaching out to hold Goldie's hand, presumably to let her know that she wasn't alone. She shifted away, her guard still just about strong enough to repel his kindness. "Has he given any indications about who might've assisted him today?"

"He's saying nothing," Christina said. "And I mean nothing. We managed to identify him through his fingerprints, but he wouldn't even confirm his name when asked."

"But he's not acting alone, right?" Zeke said. "Someone probably hired him to kill Goldie and told him exactly when to target her."

"It seems like he's working with an insider to share the two-million-dollar reward." Christina looked squarely at Goldie. "Goldie can't stay here any longer. She's been compromised."

Garth shook his head in disagreement. "I spoke to my most trusted informant this morning, and he told me that Goldie was reported to have been spotted in Santa Fe by a pickpocket. It was probably just a woman who looked like her, but it was enough to get all the bounty hunters converging on the city. They're convinced she's in New Mexico. This Marty Foster guy would appear to be the only person who's got access to inside information, and now that he's in custody Goldie should be safe again."

"Our inside informer will almost certainly find another bad guy to fill Marty's shoes," Christina said. "Goldie will never be safe here. She has to leave."

"The question we desperately need to answer," Karl said, entering the conversation, "is how did Foster find out Goldie was here? Who is our informer?"

"Let's look at the evidence," Christina replied. "In our quest to find out as much about this ex-marine as possible, we came across one very interesting piece of information. Three years ago, just after he got out of prison, Foster was arrested for a home invasion and he successfully fought the charge in court. His slippery lawyer managed to get the charges dismissed."

Zeke gasped. "You've got to be kidding me!" he exclaimed, taking a likely guess. "The lawyer was Willy Murphy?"

Christina pointed at him. "Bingo."

"Well, that sure is interesting," Goldie said with a slow nod. "There's a proven link between my attacker and Mrs. Volto's lawyer."

"We have to consider the possibility that this is simply a coincidence," Christina said. "Willy Murphy is one of the most successful lawyers in Philadelphia, so it's not unusual for a criminal like Foster to be associated with him. Their connection may be entirely innocent."

"Or it may be a sign that Willy is hoping to

pocket that two-million-dollar reward," Zeke said. "We need to interview him."

Christina's expression was doubtful. "What we have is entirely circumstantial. Willy would tear us apart if we implied he was involved in criminal activity without solid evidence to back it up. He'd probably sue the Bureau for tarnishing his reputation. Let's keep this under our hats for now but be extra vigilant. Whoever covered the CCTV camera, tampered with the air-conditioning and put the dummy in the pool knows the house well and was able to cover his tracks. He was also able to access the garage with a key, so that means he could have a close link to Mrs. Volto. But Willy was at court today so that rules him out. If you see anyone acting suspiciously, report it, no matter who it is." She suddenly raised her chin toward a vent and closed her eyes. "Ahh, I think I feel the air-conditioning beginning to work. I'll be taking a moment to enjoy this." She waved a hand through the air. "Talk among yourselves for a little while."

Goldie looked across at Zeke, her mind full of worries about who she could trust in this law enforcement team. If Willy was selling her out, should she warn Mrs. Volto? A man prepared to betray a woman for two million dollars surely couldn't be trusted around a baby.

"Don't look so worried," Zeke whispered, while Karl and Garth held a deep and serious conversation next to him. "You'll be fine."

"How can you say that?" Her stomach was in knots. "Nothing is fine."

"Remember what I said earlier about putting in more effort to help you?" he said. "Well, I'd like to make good on that promise. I'd like to be assigned to your next safe house."

"Really?" She was shocked. "You'd do that for me?"

"Of course. You need good friends in your life, Goldie, people who'll help you figure out a way to build up your self-esteem." He smiled. "I want to be one of those people. I'd like to help you find your faith again without being patronizing or flippant, because it's a long road ahead, right?"

Did he have any idea exactly how long the road was? Goldie wondered. She would likely never leave the Witness Protection Program. She'd be in it for the rest of her life.

"My life is about to be turned on its head," she said. "I'll never go back to my home in Philly, or back to the office, or back to my job. It's nice that you want to help me, Zeke, but you have a life of your own to go back to in New York."

"I know." He glanced at the others in the room, apparently not wanting to be overheard. Christina was in a world of her own, standing with her arms outstretched by the air vent while Karl and Garth argued about whether Marty Foster should be on a twenty-four-hour cell watch. "Arrangements for new lives and identities can take months, sometimes years. While you wait for those details to be finalized, I'd like to be on your protection team. It would give us more time together, for us to draw a line beneath the past and allow you to heal."

She imagined how it might be to share a home with Zeke, to cook together, or watch TV in the evenings and sit in the yard on a sunny day. It was the vision she always used to carry with her, the dream she'd held on to for such a long time even after they lost each other.

"I don't think it would work out," she said. "Every time we talk about our history, we fight. Do you seriously think our situation would change if you stayed with me longer? We're never going to get over this hurdle of me needing an apology." She dropped her voice to a whisper. "I know that the blame lies with my dad rather than you, but he never took responsibility for anything. You were right when you said that I've been projecting all my frustrations onto you. It's not fair, but I don't know how to stop. It's like I can't move on without someone telling me they're sorry."

He exhaled, long and steady, as if weighing his options.

"If I apologize for the past, will you allow me to request a reassignment to your safe house?"

"I don't want to force you into making an apology that you don't want to give," she replied. "Believe it or not, I respect you too much for that."

"How about you let me make that choice?"

"Sure. If that's what you want."

"It's what I want."

He closed his eyes, laced his fingers and used the platform to rest his chin, suddenly lost in thought, as if contemplating his next move.

Whatever path he decided, Goldie figured that they had a bumpy road ahead. Because she and Zeke couldn't agree on anything without arguing about it first.

EIGHT

Zeke walked into the kitchen, yawning and stretching in the strong morning light that had permeated the drapes across the window. His night had been fretful, full of bad dreams about his old church back in New York. Susan had been looming over him, demanding an apology while the pastor stood silently by, head bowed in shame. Zeke had awoken in a cold sweat, questioning whether his subconscious was warning him against making the same mistake again. Heartache was bound to follow.

But if he wanted to be with Goldie beyond this assignment, there was no other option.

"Good morning, Agent Miller," Karl said, looking up from his newspaper on the kitchen counter. "The news outlets are full of speculation about the likely outcome of the Volto trial after the sensational testimony of Mrs. Volto. I have a strong feeling we're going to get a guilty verdict in a few weeks' time. The signs are good."

"Let's hope so. A man like Leonardo Volto deserves to be put behind bars. Can you believe that he threatened to cut his wife into a thousand pieces and mail them to her father?" He poured himself a coffee from the steaming pot. "When Mrs. Volto told us that her husband would never hurt their baby, I guess she was lying not only to us but also to herself."

Karl leaned across the counter, checking the doorway for listening ears. "Between you and me, I don't think Leonardo Volto is an abusive husband. He's abused plenty of others, but he's always been fiercely protective of his wife, especially since her pregnancy." He dropped his voice to a whisper. "I think Mrs. Volto wanted to present herself as a victim so she embellished a few details."

"You mean she lied."

Karl made a face as though he were sucking a cut lemon. "If a little white lie gives her a more sympathetic character, then it all works in our favor. She was a superb witness for the prosecution. Highly credible."

Zeke clamped his mouth shut. Telling a little white lie while under oath wasn't something he would ever condone, no matter how evil the defendant. A fair trial required honesty at each step of the way. But he wasn't in charge of this case, and he needed Karl on his side for his next request.

"Sir," he said, putting down his cup on the counter. "I have a favor to ask."

"Shoot."

"I wondered if I could be allocated to Goldie's protection case once this assignment is over. She's going to need trained agents to accompany her to the safe house and guard her while she's there."

Karl took off his glasses and placed them on his paper, pursing his lips. His body language didn't bode well.

"Why would you want to do that, Zeke?" he asked. "You'd only be delaying the inevitable. It would make your final goodbye even worse than it would be now. My advice to you is go back to New York and get on with your life."

"I can't do that, sir. I need to make sure Goldie is safe."

"She *is* safe. She's safe with the Bureau. We'll take good care of her and make sure she has everything she needs. You should remember that we're experts at this."

"But she needs me specifically, sir. Goldie and I have grown close, and I'd like to stay with her a little longer if I may, to help her deal with some issues."

"Oh Zeke," Karl said with a sigh. "I understand that you're trying to help, but this isn't the way to go about it. We try to discourage people in the Witness Protection Program from retaining ties with their old lives. It prevents them from fully breaking with the past."

"Do you think that Goldie will definitely require a new identity? Is there no chance she could go into hiding for a while and wait for the heat to die down? If the Volto brothers get long sentences, the hit on Goldie will be old news in a few months."

Karl gave a wry smile. "That's wishful thinking, Zeke. You know as well as I do that a Mafia hit never expires. There will be a price on her head forever." He folded up his paper, obviously carefully considering his next words. "She'll need intensive counseling to enable her to adjust to becoming a new person. It's a long, hard road ahead, and she needs to leave all her baggage behind." He raised his eyebrows. "Do you understand what I mean?"

That forced Zeke to think deeply. What was best for Goldie? Would she be better off without the baggage he would inevitably bring?

"I need some time to fully consider this," he said. "When do you think I'll be required to return to New York?"

"Now that Mrs. Volto has given her testimony, we'll be removing her protection detail, but I'll offer her one last opportunity to enter the Witness Protection Program. If she declines, which I have no doubt she will, we'll close her case file, withdraw our agents and allow her to employ private bodyguards."

"When do you expect to pull out?"

"Tomorrow. Mrs. Volto is fully aware of our plans, so I'm guessing she already has private security lined up. You'll almost certainly be leaving Philadelphia tomorrow afternoon."

Zeke swallowed away a sour taste in his mouth. He could be headed back to New York in a little over twenty-four hours. These might be his last precious moments with Goldie before they were forced apart yet again.

Karl noticed his discomfort. "If you decide that you really do want to accompany Goldie to her next safe house, I'll approve it with her and put in an official request, but I'll need to know by eight o'clock this evening. Time is of the essence here, Zeke. Christina will be moving Goldie out of here tomorrow morning, whether you're on the assignment or not."

He calculated the time he had left to make what could amount to the most important decision of his life: eleven hours.

"Thank you, sir. I'll give it some serious consideration."

"Serious consideration?" Goldie said, breezing into the room, her ankle seemingly now able to bear her weight without causing her to wince. "That sounds ominous."

"We're just discussing something important," Zeke said. "Something that needs quite a lot of thought."

Karl tucked his newspaper beneath his arm before sliding from his stool. "It's another hot one out there, and we've had warnings of potential blackouts later due to the strain on the grid. I'll just go check with Christina that we have contingency plans in place." He smiled. "I'll leave you guys alone. I'm sure you have a lot to discuss."

Goldie watched him leave the kitchen, her expression bemused as she took a carton of juice from the fridge. "What did he mean by that?"

"I asked him if it was possible to reassign me to your protection detail. He said he needs a firm decision later this evening."

"Oh." She stood, holding the juice in mid-air. "And what will you decide?"

"I'm not sure. I want to come with you, but Karl thinks it's not in your best interest."

She raised an eyebrow skeptically. "Really?"

"Yes, really. Once you enter the Witness Protection Program, all your focus should go into choosing and learning about your new life. I might hold you back."

She put the juice back in the fridge and roughly closed the door. "It sounds to me like you're simply looking for an easy way to withdraw your offer."

"No, that's got nothing to do with it. I want what's best for you, Goldie."

"And you don't think that maintaining a relationship with me is a good thing?"

"Not in the long run, no."

"Just admit it, Zeke," she said, folding her arms. "You changed your mind. You don't have to lie to me."

"I'm not lying. I think I'm falling for you all over again, Goldie. I would never lie to you."

She froze, staring at him, as the weight of his declaration seemed to take full effect.

"You should never say a thing like that unless you mean it," she said quietly.

"I do mean it. The only reason I'm undecided about accompanying you to your safe house is because it might end up hurting you in the end. What if I come with you and we find ourselves growing even closer? What if we end up as besotted as we used to be?"

"Do you really think that might happen? It doesn't seem likely."

"It seems highly likely to me. What if we found ourselves head over heels in love?" He touched her forearm. "Would you ever consider allowing me to enter the Witness Protection Program with you? If that were a possibility?"

"That's a ridiculous question, Zeke," she replied quickly. "It's such a monumental step to take, to give up everything you've ever known, especially when you don't need to. I don't know why you'd even contemplate it."

He didn't miss a beat. "Because I want to be with you."

"You can't be sure of that, not really."

He fell silent. She was almost certainly correct. How could he be sure that he wanted to leave behind his life, family and friends to start over with Goldie? He had a good life in New York with everything he'd ever wanted. Everything except her.

He placed a flat palm across his heart.

"Something is telling me that my place is by your side. I don't know how to explain it, but it's like an invisible thread is joining me to you. Wherever you go, I want to follow."

"That's a sweet idea, but it's little more than a fantasy," she said. "You've had enough experience of the Witness Protection Program to know that it's psychologically damaging for plenty of people. Adjusting to a new name and new identity takes its toll, and it's a decision that should never be taken lightly. Don't even think about it."

He knew she was right. Some people in WITSEC never fully integrated into their new lives and continually hankered for the old, sometimes even returning to their hometowns in spite of the serious danger. Zeke was under no illusions about the implications of what he was asking. He just needed to know that it was a choice, because the only other option was letting her go, and that seemed even worse in comparison.

"What if I want to think about it?" he asked. "I know it must seem like a crazy idea but won't you at least consider it?"

"I have to be realistic," she said. "I couldn't let you give up your life for me. It's way too much for anybody to ask of a person." Her face fell with an expression of profound sadness. "I think you're a good person who tries really hard to do the right thing, and I appreciate everything you've done for me here. But it's time for me to finally admit that we were never destined to be together. I think there was still a small part of me that hoped you'd apologize for hurting me, sweep me into your arms and make everything all better." She smiled weakly. "But I have to stop living in a ridiculous fantasy world. You and I will never get back together. Tomorrow you'll be out of my life, and we can both finally close the book on whatever we had."

He didn't think it was possible to close their book. The ending was yet to be written.

"You said that if I apologized for not trying harder to find you all those years ago, then you'd allow me onto your safe house protection detail." He was still hopeful of salvaging something positive out of this. "Does that still stand?"

"Does it really matter?" she asked with a weary sigh as she turned to leave the kitchen. "It'll never happen anyway."

Zeke scrolled through the list of contacts on his cell phone, found the one he needed and hit the call button. He was still unsure of what he wanted to say, or why. He only knew that he had to find out the answers to some very important questions.

The voice on the line hadn't changed at all over the last three years, and in his mind Zeke saw a big, bearded, smiling face saying, "Hello, this is Pastor Jim."

"Hi, Jim. It's Zeke."

"Zeke!" Jim sounded pleasantly surprised. "It's great to hear from you. How are you, buddy?"

"Not so great right now. I'm on assignment, but I've hit a snag and I need some help. I have some questions."

"Sure. Go ahead."

He may as well come right out with it. "Why didn't you believe me when I said that I saw Susan steal from the church collection plate? Why did you insist on asking me to apologize when there was nothing to apologize for? Why did you let her get away with it and punish me by allowing me to leave the congregation instead of her?"

Jim was silent for a few seconds, as if formulating a response.

Finally, he said, "When you saw Susan steal from the collection plate, it wasn't the first time she'd done it. She admitted to me that she'd stolen from us four times previously. I knew you were telling the truth, and

I also knew I was placing a lot of pressure on your shoulders when asking you to apologize."

This was a lot for Zeke to take in. Jim had known all along that his apology had been hollow. So why force him to make it?

"Will you explain to me exactly what happened?" Zeke asked. "I think I deserve that at least."

"I can be open with you now. Susan passed away eight months ago, so she doesn't need me to keep her secrets any longer."

Zeke was shocked. "I'm so sorry. I didn't realize Susan had died." He guessed that she hadn't even reached sixty years of age. "I don't want to cause you any distress, Jim."

"That's okay, Zeke. She's at peace with the Lord now, and it sounds like you need some closure on what happened."

"Yes, I do, if it's possible."

"Susan was very sick when she stole from church, and she was trying to save enough money for a doctor's appointment to find out what was wrong. She had no health insurance, you see, and she was too embarrassed to ask us for help."

"She was embarrassed?" Jim's church was the most supportive and caring Zeke had ever known. "There's no shame in being sick."

"Do you recall the Bible story about the woman who touched Jesus's cloak and was healed of her affliction?"

Zeke recalled the passage from the gospels. "Sure. She'd been bleeding for twelve years, I think."

"That's right. Susan had been bleeding in the same way and for an awfully long time, and she was experiencing the same sense of shame and embarrassment that the woman in the Bible must have endured. She was a shy person and couldn't bring herself to tell any members of the church what was happening to her. She needed money to explore the reason for her bleeding, so she took it from the church. What you saw was a desperate woman who stole from the only person she trusted with her secret—God."

Zeke leaned against the wall in his bedroom and ran a hand down his face. "Why didn't you tell me this at the time, Jim? It would've helped me to understand why she did it." He burned with disgrace at the way he had judged her harshly at the time. "I was so angry at being forced to make an apology for being mistaken in what I saw. I couldn't get past the unfairness of it."

"Susan begged me not to tell anybody what she'd done, and I agreed because she needed the love and protection of the church. And I couldn't expose her illness to anybody either. I gave her my word."

"So you sacrificed me instead?"

"I guess I did, but sometimes we have to make these hard choices. You're strong, Zeke. You're someone who can eat everything, whereas others can eat only vegetables."

"What?"

"Romans chapter fourteen. It tells us that we mustn't pass judgment on those whose faith is weak. People like you, with unshakable faith, can eat everything on the table, but people like Susan, whose faith is weak, can eat only vegetables. I knew you could withstand the sacrifice I was asking of you because you're a strong man of God."

Zeke fell silent, considering all that Jim had divulged. This changed everything. Susan hadn't been brazenly stealing for the purposes of greed. She had been trying to touch the cloak of Jesus, and Zeke could have ruined her reputation had he not withdrawn from the church without making a fuss.

"Zeke," Jim said. "Are you still there?"

"Yeah, I'm still here. I'm sorry, Jim. I'm sorry for not realizing that you must've had a good reason for asking me to apologize even though I had done nothing wrong. I'm glad you sacrificed me. It was the right thing to do, and I hope Susan got the help she needed."

"She was eventually diagnosed with advanced uterine cancer, but the church helped with the medical expenses and we formed an action team to take care of her around the clock. She passed peacefully in the end, and I'm glad to say that her faith grew stronger and stronger as her body grew weaker."

"I'm pleased about that. Thank you, Jim. You're a good man."

"*You* are a good man, Zeke. You never once considered exposing her sin of stealing to the other members of the church. You simply left quietly, and I was really sorry to see you go. Would you consider rejoining us?"

Zeke smiled. "I would love to rejoin you. I've missed you guys more than you could ever know."

"That's great news."

Then he remembered his predicament. "But I'm not sure I'll be returning to New York. I met someone special and the situation is complicated."

"I see. Would you like to tell me about her?"

"She's someone who only eats vegetables."

"I assume you're not talking literally here."

"I wish I was." Zeke sighed deeply. "I don't

know what to do, Jim. I usually have such a strong sense of what path to take ahead of me, but this time I'm clueless. I want to be with her, but I don't know what's in her best interest. Plus she wants me to apologize for something that isn't my fault."

Jim laughed a little. "That seems to be a running theme in your life, huh? Are you going to give her the apology?"

"I didn't intend to," he said. "But things seem a lot different now. I think she's worth the sacrifice."

"Whatever you decide to do, Zeke, you'll always be in my prayers."

"And you in mine, Jim."

He hung up the phone and sat on his bed to reflect on all that he'd just learned. Hearing Jim's voice again had been uplifting, reminding him of what was awaiting him in New York. He would be able to rejoin the church he loved, to connect with the members he'd missed for the last three years. His new church was perfectly adequate for his needs, but this was like finding your family in the wilderness after wandering alone.

Yet Goldie needed him too. She was facing certain danger, and her faith was weak to the point of nonexistence. He could be her strength, the person who was prepared to dig in for the long haul and not flee at the first sign of difficulty.

He just needed to figure out if it was the right thing to do.

Goldie allowed the tears to fall without brushing them away, and they splashed in big, fat drops onto the page of her open Bible. Someone had once told her that God couldn't truly mold people until they had been broken. Well, Goldie felt herself to be well and truly broken, no longer able to fight or pretend to be tough. Inside, she was tired and weak and scared, facing an uncertain future without Zeke by her side.

Having convinced herself she had gotten over her first and only love, Zeke's shock reappearance in her life had served as a powerful reminder that he was and would always be her hero. And she wanted him with her. But there was no way he could or should enter the Witness Protection Program. He had a great life in New York, with a loving family and a solid career path. What could she offer him in return for that?

A knock sounded on the door. It was bound to be Zeke. It was only ever him. She placed the Bible on the bed beside her and walked to the door, passing the suitcase she had packed in preparation for her transfer to a new safe house the following morning.

Unlocking the door, she opened up to see Zeke standing there, hands shoved deep into the pockets of his jeans, his white shirt crumpled and untucked. Smiling a little awkwardly and with a hopeful raise of an eyebrow, she couldn't deny that he was gorgeous.

"There's a little party going on downstairs," he said. "To celebrate Mrs. Volto's successful day on the witness stand. The newspapers are full of praise for the brave mobster's wife risking her safety for the sake of her unborn baby."

"That's great," she said. "You all deserve some downtime."

"You wanna join us?"

"No, thanks, I'm a little preoccupied right now."

"Is everything all right? You've been shut away in here all by yourself for hours."

"I'm fine," she said, quickly wiping the streaks from her face. "I just needed some quiet time to prepare myself for leaving tomorrow." She opened the door wide to allow him to enter. "I finally got around to reading that Bible you gave me."

His eyes strayed to the open pages. "Is it helping?"

"Actually, it is." She sat on the bed. "God loves a weak spirit, right?"

He sat next to her. "Of course, because when we're at our weakest, He's at his strongest."

"Oh boy. God must have superstrength right now, because my weakness knows no bounds, but I'm learning to have faith." In the depths of her misery, a tiny seed had been planted, one that she sensed was good and strong. "Giving up control is so hard, Zeke, but I have no choice. The fight has gone out of me."

He took her hand and held it for a few seconds, gently sweeping his thumb over her knuckles.

"I'm sorry," he said. "I'm sorry for hurting you and for not doing more to try to find you when you vanished from Glenside. I'm sorry for not acknowledging my blame sooner. You deserved an apology and I made you wait. And for that, I'm the sorriest of all."

She laughed, hiccuping slightly. "You don't owe me an apology, Zeke. You never did. I was hurt and angry, and I needed to pin the blame on somebody. Neither of us did anything wrong, and what happened was nobody's fault except my father's." She dropped her eyes, shamefaced. "I bullied you into apologizing, and that was wrong of me."

"I'd apologize a million times over if it would make you happy again," he said. "I wish I'd come right out with it the first time you asked, instead of getting defensive."

"You're a sweet and kind and lovely man, Zeke, and you'll make a very fortunate lady an awesome husband one day." She stopped for a moment to wait for her heart to settle. "Promise me that when you go back to New York, you'll enjoy your life and find somebody special to share it with. You deserve that."

"What I really want to do is come to the next safe house with you, Goldie. Karl said that if I give him my decision by eight o'clock this evening, he could get me onto the list of assigned agents." He checked his watch. "It's only five."

After Zeke had been so selfless, now it was Goldie's turn to repay the kindness. If Zeke accompanied her after leaving this house, there was a very good chance that he would ultimately sacrifice his life in New York in order to remain with her forever. They both knew the strength of their bond, and it was almost impossible to break. But only almost.

"I don't want you to come with me, Zeke,"

she said. "When you said that it might not be in my best interest, you were right. I have to make a clean break with my past, and that includes you."

"But what if I want to be part of your future?" he asked. "What if I want to make a clean break too and start over with you?" He smiled. "Think of it as the adventure we missed out on when we were younger. We could make up for those twenty-one years that we spent apart."

She stood up, needing to put some space between them in case his gentle coaxing persuaded her to change her mind. What Zeke was suggesting was a huge deal, one that he hadn't truly considered. She couldn't ask him to leave behind everything he'd ever known.

"You're not listening to me," she said. "I don't want you to come with me. I want to go into the Witness Protection Program alone. I'm only just starting to deal with the emotional problems in my life and, like you said, there's a long road ahead. I might not be fully healed for years. I'm a work in progress."

"I don't care. I'll take you as you are, Goldie. I don't expect or want you to change."

"What if you leave everything behind to be with me and later regret it? You can't just go back to your old life and pick up where you left off. You'd be stuck with a new identity, with a new life and with no way out."

He stood to stand close to her. "What if I leave everything behind and never regret it?" he asked. "Have you considered that possibility too?"

"No, because the odds are stacked against us, Zeke. You know how hard it is for people to adjust to new lives in the Witness Protection Program. Some of them never fully integrate and they end up miserable and lonely and oftentimes try to return to the things they used to know, no matter the risk. I refuse to put you in that position. I won't let you come with me. I should never have even considered it."

His brow wrinkled as if slowly breaking. "Won't you at least let me try? If I stayed with you for a while, you could give it a little more thought. You're not thinking straight right now."

Her eyes strayed to the open Bible. "I'm thinking straight for the first time in my life." She sat down again, weary and drained. "I've been really selfish and treated you badly, so it's time for me to step up and do the right thing. I want you to go home and be with your family and friends and church. In comparison to all of those things, I can't offer you anything."

"What are you talking about?" he asked incredulously. "You're all I ever wanted in my life."

"No, Zeke, you're looking through rose-colored glasses. We don't really know each other anymore. It's been twenty-one years since we were last together, and five days isn't enough time for either of us to assess whether we have a future."

"It's enough time for me," he said quietly.

She stood abruptly and walked to the door, feeling the need to bring this conversation to a close.

"I've made my decision." She held the door open. "And I'd like some time to pray about it."

Zeke stood in the center of the room for a few seconds before heading out into the hallway.

"Sometimes, our first instinct isn't always the right one," he said. "I literally just learned that. There's still time to change your mind."

Goldie didn't want to hear it. Her mind was already made up, and she just needed to shore up her defenses for the goodbye she would have to endure in the morning.

"You've been really good to me over these

last few days, Zeke," she said, closing the door on everything they'd once had. "But we're done."

Goldie rooted through the cabinet in the bathroom to find the face cream she'd left there five days previously. Five days was all it had taken to irrevocably upend her life, reconnecting her with a boy she'd once loved and lost and forcing her to accept that a price of two million dollars would be forever on her head.

What else could now go wrong before she was due to leave this house in the morning?

Finding the jar of cream, she slid it into her toiletries bag and zipped it up, ready to be easily put into her suitcase when she awoke. She wasn't sure what time she was due to leave, but Christina said it would be early. That suited her just fine. No long, drawn-out goodbyes with Zeke and no time to consider whether she truly knew what she was doing.

"It's the right thing to do," she muttered under her breath. "You have to set him free."

Checking her reflection, she groaned at the disheveled mess in the mirror, took a deep breath and walked out into the hallway. She heard the sounds of laughter downstairs accompanied by the clink of cutlery on china plates. Since the news stations and papers had begun to focus on a likely guilty verdict for the Volto brothers, Mrs. Volto had been in high spirits, spending a lot of time on the telephone, seemingly making travel arrangements to take a vacation, while Willy grinned like a Cheshire cat. Goldie had remained in her bedroom for the evening, with no appetite or desire to join the party. Zeke had tried to persuade her, but she couldn't bear to see his face any longer. This was hard enough already.

Going back into her room, she clicked the door closed and leaned against it, resting her head on the wood. Was it too early to go to bed? Would she simply lie awake and be tormented by her thoughts?

Pulling back the duvet, she retrieved her pajamas from beneath her pillow, but before she had a chance to get changed, the room was plunged into darkness. The voices from below became loud and animated as Goldie felt around in the dark, heading to what she hoped was the door.

A beeping began to sound from somewhere in the vicinity, a little like a muffled alarm clock, rhythmic, quiet but high-pitched.

"Zeke!" she shouted, stumbling into the

wall and feeling her way around. "There's something in here!"

She found the handle, turned and pulled. It was locked. Or jammed. Yanking with all her strength, she shouted again, as the beeping worked its way up to a crescendo. She was in trouble.

"Zeke!" she yelled at the top of her lungs. "I need you!"

NINE

Zeke raced upstairs in the dark, heading toward the sound of Goldie's panicked voice. She was pounding on the door, shouting, calling his name.

"I'm here," he yelled, turning the handle. "Unlock the door."

"I can't. The key is gone."

"What's going on?"

"I can't get out, Zeke, and I think there's a bomb in here."

"Stand back from the door."

He brought up his foot and kicked the door with a heavy blow. It gave way instantly, and Goldie practically fell into his arms at the same time as a flash lit up the entire room, like lightning across a night sky. The explosion ripped through the air, blowing them off their feet and onto the carpet of the landing, where they lay in a tangle of limbs. Goldie screamed and buried her head in Zeke's neck, while Garth tried to pull them both from the flames that had taken hold in the bedroom and were licking the frame of the door, just inches away from their feet.

Zeke coughed and spluttered but refused to let go of Goldie in his arms as the smoke alarm began to screech overhead. He somehow managed to stagger to his feet, holding her tight, and move her a few feet away, where her limbs suddenly went slack with her unconsciousness.

Karl rushed past with a fire extinguisher and battled the flames as best he could while shouting for Garth to take everybody downstairs and call the fire department.

"Come on, Zeke," Garth said, yanking on his shirt. "Let's get Goldie out of here."

Lifting her off her feet, Zeke carried her in his arms down the stairs toward a flashlight being held by Mrs. Volto, who was standing next to Willy.

"Lay her on the couch," Mrs. Volto said, lighting the way into the living room. "Is she okay?"

"She's fine," Zeke said, laying her down and tapping her hand to rouse her. "Can I borrow your flashlight?"

Mrs. Volto handed it over, and Zeke lifted

up one of Goldie's eyelids to shine the beam beneath.

"Her pupils are dilating as normal," he said, running his hands gently down her arms and legs, checking for any breaks. "She's been knocked out by the blast. That's all."

"Whatever happened?" Mrs. Volto said, holding tight to Willy's hand. "What caused that explosion?"

"It was a bomb," Zeke said, shining the flashlight around them, looking for something, anything that might be a clue. "Somebody got inside and planted a bomb." The beam picked out the faces of Garth, Mrs. Volto and Willy. "It could even be one of you. We're totally in the dark here in more ways than one."

"The fire department is on its way," Garth said. "But you need to go to the back of the house and close the inner doors until the fire is out, to prevent smoke inhalation." He put a hand on Zeke's shoulder. "You stay with Goldie while I help Karl. Take her out back and don't let her out of your sight. You can't leave her on her own, not even for a second. You understand?"

"I understand," Zeke replied, lifting her into his arms once again. "She's not safe with anybody but me."

* * *

The acrid smell of smoke hung in the air, clinging to every fiber and surface. The firefighters had fully extinguished the flames, and experts were now analyzing the remains of the bomb in Goldie's bedroom, deciphering how it was made and by whom. But with the power still out, progress was slow and they would likely be there through the night. As the minutes ticked by, the temperature crept up, no longer cooled by the electricity-reliant air-conditioning, and the atmosphere became muggy, like a tropical rain forest.

Zeke sat next to Goldie in the kitchen, his body as close to hers as possible. Having been examined and cleared by a paramedic, she was permitted to take part in this final meeting of the Volto case team before it would be disbanded the following day.

"Listen up," Christina said, addressing the four other people in the room. "This level of attack is unprecedented so we're disseminating information on a need-to-know basis. Goldie's in serious danger, and we need to get her out of here as soon as possible. I've ordered a car to come get her immediately. It should be here in about an hour."

"One hour?" Zeke knew their time was

short, but this was something else. "That's all we have?"

"We have no choice." Christina's anxious face was lit by the soft glow of tens of candles around the room. "This situation is getting worse by the second. Just over an hour ago, Marty Foster was found dead in his jail cell."

"No way!" Zeke could scarcely believe it. "How?"

"He hung himself with his bootlaces," Karl said with a skeptical raise of an eyebrow. "The Philadelphia Police Department considers it a suicide."

Garth gave a snort of disbelief. "How come his bootlaces weren't taken from him by the desk sergeant?"

"The desk sergeant says he confiscated his laces, his wallet and keys, his jewelry and anything else that he might use to harm himself," Karl replied. "But somehow, those bootlaces found their way from an evidence bag into the cell. I've asked the coroner to perform a full autopsy. Something's wrong here, and I think the police are trying to cover up their mistakes."

"Somebody murdered him," Zeke said. "They needed to keep him from talking, so they killed him."

Christina nodded. "That's my theory too.

Mr. Foster had requested a meeting with me tomorrow morning, and I think he was ready to strike a deal, but now we'll never know."

"Who had access to his cell?" Zeke asked. "There must be camera footage."

"You won't be surprised to learn that the camera footage has been lost. Someone deleted the files before we managed to get hold of them."

"Surely we have a list of suspects." Zeke was beginning to wonder exactly how many people were betraying them. This level of chaos could not be the work of just one person. "The culprit has to be a member of law enforcement, either FBI or police."

"Foster was being held at the Philly PD headquarters, one of the busiest stations in the entire state. The desk sergeant said that numerous officers came and went during the window of opportunity. He's not been able to offer us a great deal of help, but he's trying to protect the reputation of the force. The police allowed an arrested man to be murdered on their watch, and the sergeant simply wants the investigation to go away."

"The FBI will take over the investigation into Foster's death, right?" Zeke asked. "There's a serious breach in this case, possibly from multiple sources. We've been coming under attack since the very first day Goldie and I arrived, and now a man has been murdered in police custody. Something is very seriously wrong here." He looked across at Goldie. "I don't know if it's safe for Goldie to leave right now."

"Well, it sure isn't safe for her to stay," Christina said. "Her bedroom just exploded."

"And that's another breach," Zeke said. "Who put that bomb in Goldie's room? How and when did they get the opportunity?"

"The early reports from the forensics guys suggest that the bomb worked on a timer switch and could've been placed inside her wardrobe at any point during the day. It was a homemade device, not particularly sophisticated but powerful, and it was intended to kill anybody in the room. Goldie was fortunate to be able to get out in time." Christina leaned across the table toward Zeke. "Are you sure that the door was locked on the outside? Could it have been jammed or stuck?"

Goldie now spoke up. "It was locked. I'm sure of it. The key is always in the lock but it was gone. Somebody locked the door right after I went inside."

As she spoke, Zeke noticed that she was pale and downcast, as if she'd given up. It was unbearable to see her like this.

"Goldie's right," he said. "She was trapped, and I got to her with only a second to spare. I think somebody activated the bomb as soon as the lights went out, hoping to capitalize on the sudden darkness."

"Who had the opportunity to place the bomb in her room and remove the key?" Garth asked.

Christina checked off the people on her fingers. "You, Karl, Zeke, Mrs. Volto and Willy."

"Unless somebody is getting inside without us knowing," Karl said ominously.

Christina shook her head. "The procedures for getting in and out of this house are airtight. There's no way anybody could gain access without authorization."

"Actually," Zeke began, "that's not entirely true."

Goldie shot him a look of concern, warning him against revealing the secret they had both promised to keep.

"What are you talking about, Agent Miller?" Christina asked in a tone that demanded truth. "Who's been coming into the house without authorization?"

"Goldie caught Willy Murphy in Mrs. Volto's bedroom during the night, but he wasn't on the official overnight list. Mrs.

Volto admitted that she sometimes signed him out of the house in the evening but, instead of leaving, Willy would stay in her bedroom until the morning. Then he would sign back into the house and pretend that he'd only just arrived, when in reality, he'd never actually left."

Christina was confused. "But why would Mrs. Volto hide her lawyer in her bedroom overnight?" Her face broke into an expression of surprise as realization dawned. "Oh! She's in an intimate relationship with him?"

"Yes," Zeke replied. "And she was desperate to keep it all under wraps in case her husband found out. Her baby is the only thing protecting her right now, but if Leonardo thinks it's not his child…" He let the unsaid words hang in the air.

"I see." Christina's eyes darted back and forth across the table, clearly agitated by this news. "If Willy was able to stay overnight without following the correct protocol, then it would appear that my airtight procedures aren't so airtight after all." She rose from her chair. "It makes me wonder who else has gotten inside without us knowing. I think I need to have a conversation with Mrs. Volto to see if there are any other rules of entry she's been bending. Karl, shall we go together?"

"Sure." Karl stood up. "Zeke, don't let Goldie out of your sight until the car arrives to transport her to a new safe house. I didn't receive your official request to reassign to her protection detail, so I assume you changed your mind."

"He did," Goldie said quietly. "I'm fine to go by myself."

"I've arranged for two female agents to accompany you to your new place," Karl said. "And Christina has ordered some new clothes to replace the ones that were destroyed." He smiled. "It'll be a regular home away from home."

As Karl and Christina left the room, Garth cleared his throat and pushed back his chair. "I'll go see if the forensics guys could use my help."

All three knew that this was a convenient excuse to give them some space, and Zeke was so very grateful to Garth for excusing himself at that moment. He and Goldie would shortly be saying goodbye, and the time that remained was precious.

"Listen to me, Goldie," he said, moving his chair to face hers. "We don't have a lot of time, but I think I can persuade Karl to allow me to come with you if you'll allow it."

"That subject is no longer up for discussion."

"But you shouldn't have to go alone."

She smiled. "I won't be alone, Zeke. I feel my faith slowly returning, and wherever I go, I know I won't ever be alone."

He took her hand, their skin dancing with flickering light from the candles. "I'm really pleased that you're finding your belief again, but there's room in your life for both God and me, isn't there?"

She pushed her hair from her face and held it back with her hand. "There is so much damage from my past that I have to deal with—my father's crimes, my mom's death, losing touch with my sister when she moved overseas, my loss of faith, my inability to let anyone get close to me." She paused. "And my breakup with you."

"I understand that you want to take time to recover and deal with these things," he said. "But you have to remember that nobody ever reaches a point of perfection. There will always be something that prevents you from having the perfect life. Unless you learn to be happy in the dark times, you'll never be happy at all."

She remained silent, playing with his fingers, rubbing her index finger across his wrist.

"I don't expect anything from you," he continued. "If you decide that you don't want to rekindle our relationship, then I'll accept it and leave without a fuss. All I ask is that you give us a chance. Let me come with you to your safe house where we can have a few more weeks together, to see what happens."

Her eyes began to glisten in the low light, and her mouth turned down at the corners. "What if it doesn't work out, Zeke? What if you're the one who decides to walk away? Have you ever thought of that?"

Truthfully, Zeke had never considered that possibility because he simply couldn't envision it.

"I'll never give up on you, Goldie," he said. "Never in a million years."

"Oh Zeke." She wiped away a tear. "I love your optimism, but it's so naive. Life goes wrong all the time, and invariably we don't get what we want. It could all go wrong at any second and…and…" She stopped and placed a palm across her chest. "And my heart couldn't cope with it a second time around. I'm not strong enough."

He cupped her cheek, feeling the wetness of her tears. "If fear of pain is what's holding you back, you have to let it go. Now that your faith is returning, you have a platform to stand on. You don't have to leave anything to chance because nothing is random."

He could almost see the struggle behind her eyes. "I want to agree with you, Zeke, I really do, but I'm not there yet. Don't ask me to take a chance on you, because I just can't forget how it turned out the last time."

Zeke glanced at the clock, conscious of the minutes ticking by, of the possibility that these really were the last moments he would spend with her.

"I'm not asking you to take a chance on me," he said. "I'm asking you to take a chance on *us*."

"Stop." She stood and picked up a candle from the table. "I'd like to take a shower before I leave. My hair smells smoky."

"Okay." It wasn't fair of him to put pressure on her, no matter how mistaken he thought she was. "If you use the downstairs bathroom, I'll stand guard outside the door."

"Thank you. You've been kind to me and I appreciate it."

Her tone was oddly formal and awkward, the distance between them suddenly all too obvious.

"You still have fifty minutes to consider

it," he said, following her from the kitchen. "I'm packed and ready, just in case I have to beg Karl to let me go with you."

Goldie didn't respond. She simply slipped through the door of the bathroom, shut it behind her and immediately switched on the water.

Zeke suspected she was hoping to cover the sound of her tears.

Goldie towel dried her hair and ran her fingers through the curls, hoping to prevent knots from forming. The scent of smoke permeated her jeans and T-shirt, and she wished she had access to clean clothes. Yet everything she had brought with her to Gladwyne had been blown to smithereens by the bomb. She would be starting over entirely.

Zeke knocked on the door. "You okay in there?"

"Yeah. I'll be out in a second."

Goldie had taken an extralong shower, using the rushing water to muffle the sounds of her weeping. Her candle had burned down to the wick and was now surrounded by a puddle of wax in the saucer. She knew that her time in this house was short, and it was easier to while it away in the shower than to spend it looking at Zeke's face. His idealism was very persuasive, painting a picture of possible happiness and contentment. Life didn't work that way, at least not in her experience.

Opening the door, she saw him standing on the other side, the candlelight shimmering on various surfaces in the background. At first glance he appeared to be in a glittering ballroom, holding out his hand as if inviting her to dance. But he was simply offering to lead her through the dark hallway.

"Mrs. Volto would like to talk to you," he said. "She heard that you're leaving soon, and she wanted to say goodbye."

"Where is she?"

"In the kitchen." His eyes strayed to his watch. "Your car should arrive in twenty minutes, so you don't have much time."

She nodded. Twenty minutes of conversation with Louisa Volto would stop Zeke from trying to change her mind, to prevent her from making the biggest mistake of her life. Taking his hand, she padded across the wooden floor, which was warm underfoot. Without air-conditioning the house was yet again warm and humid, but the cooler night air made it bearable.

"Hi, Mrs. Volto," she said, entering the

kitchen to see her sitting at the table, a cup of coffee in front of her. "You wanted to talk?"

"You're supposed to call me Louisa now, remember? We're friends, right?" She looked up at Zeke, who was standing by the door. "Can't we have some privacy here?"

"I'm afraid that's not possible, ma'am," Zeke said. "I must have eyes on Goldie at all times."

Mrs. Volto raised her eyebrows high. "Well, I guess you turned into a VIP, huh?"

"I'm hardly a VIP, Louisa," Goldie said. "Someone planted a bomb in my room and locked me inside."

Her face fell. "Willy and I are just devastated about that. Someone must've snuck inside the house without anyone noticing." She wrung her hands. "It's terrifying to think about what could've happened."

"You need to ensure that you have professional bodyguards ready to take over when the FBI agents leave this house," Goldie said. "You've seen what can happen when somebody is determined to cause harm, and you must take precautions to safeguard your life and your baby's. Your husband will probably be going to prison for a very long time, but that doesn't mean he can't still hurt you."

"I have security people arriving in the

morning," she said. "Please don't worry about me. You're the one in danger here, and I want to extend my sympathies."

"Thank you."

"I'll miss you, Goldie." Mrs. Volto smiled. "It's not been easy for me to make new friends since I married into the Mafia. They controlled everything in my life, including the people I saw."

"You've been very kind to me, Louisa," Goldie said. "But whatever friendship we had will have to come to an end. I'll be leaving soon."

"I wondered if we could stay in touch?" Mrs. Volto asked. "Just the odd phone call or video chat. I would like that very much."

Goldie saw Zeke take a step forward, intervening on her behalf, as she suspected he would.

"I'm sorry, ma'am, but that won't be possible. Goldie's whereabouts will be a secret. Her life is in grave danger, and there are strict rules about sharing information."

"I won't get to talk to you at all?" Mrs. Volto asked. "Once you leave here, you're gone for good?"

"I'm afraid so." She reached across and patted Mrs. Volto's hand. "You'll be fine. Once the baby is born, you'll make a ton of new friends and your life will be full again. You don't need me."

Zeke turned around and sighed, and Goldie was sure she heard him mutter, *But I need you.*

"That's a real shame," Mrs. Volto said. "I hoped we could stay friends, but if there's no way to keep in touch I guess this is goodbye."

"I guess so."

The two women stood and hugged, Goldie being careful to avoid pressing onto Mrs. Volto's protruding stomach. This very first goodbye made her quite emotional, and she blinked away yet more tears. It wasn't a good sign. If she couldn't bid farewell to Mrs. Volto without becoming upset, she stood no chance of maintaining a cool composure when leaving Zeke.

"You take extra care of this special woman, Agent Miller," Mrs. Volto said, turning to face him. "She needs your protection."

"Actually, ma'am," Zeke replied, his eyes resting on Goldie. "I'm not going with her."

"You're not?" Mrs. Volto was clearly surprised. "I thought you two were joined at the hip."

Goldie shook her head. "Not at all. Wherever I'm going, I'm going by myself."

"Well, I wish you the best." Mrs. Volto patted her hand. "You're a brave woman, Goldie. I'll let you spend your remaining time with Zeke."

Zeke remained like a sentry at the door as Mrs. Volto passed him and walked to the stairs.

"It still might not be too late," he said. "I could go speak with Karl and Christina."

"Would you stop it please?" Goldie rubbed her temples. "This is hard enough as it is."

"I just don't want you to make a decision that you'll end up regretting for the rest of your life."

"Regrets are kind of a specialty of mine," she said. "But I'd rather regret setting you free than ruining your life."

"Listen to me," he said, moving into the flickering room. "I'm really worried about you. Something really bad is going on, and we have no idea who we can trust. For all we know, Mrs. Volto put that bomb in your room and locked you inside."

Goldie laughed. "Yeah, like a pregnant woman is going to risk her baby's life by planting a bomb in her own home."

"What I'm trying to say is that you can't really trust anybody anymore. I'm pretty sure we're dealing with more than one mole working against you. You could be tracked to your new safe house, and all of this could start over again."

"Christina says that the procedures for transportation are complex, so I can't be followed."

"I'd still rather be with you."

"I asked you to let it go, Zeke."

She was clearly tired and emotional, yet he could feel a sense of indecision in her voice. She was wavering.

Sitting on a chair next to her, he said, "How do you feel about me, Goldie? I mean, how do you *really* feel?"

She stared at him, biting her lip. "When I'm with you, it's like going home after a long time away. It's warm and comfortable and safe." She laughed. "Like old slippers, I guess."

He smiled. "I'm totally happy being your old slippers."

"But you deserve more than I can give you," she argued. "You should take your freedom, Zeke. You don't have to sacrifice yourself for me."

"Sacrifices are what makes us God's children, right?" He remembered how Jim had sacrificed him in order to protect Susan. Knowing the full story, Zeke was entirely at peace with it, just as he was now at peace with leaving his life behind in order to be with Goldie. "God expects us to give up important things for the sake of people we love. It shows that we care, that we're prepared to serve others before ourselves. I know you want to do this alone, but my heart is telling me that I should be serving you."

"It is?" The indecision appeared to be growing. "You want to serve me?"

"Always."

Her gaze ran back and forth along the tiles of the floor as she clearly wrestled with her conscience. She wanted to give him his freedom but, in reality, he wanted to give up everything just for the chance to be with her.

"No, Zeke," she said finally. "I have to be strong and do the right thing." She took a deep breath and stood up. "I don't want to talk about this anymore, okay?"

He sighed, sensing he was so close to a breakthrough, but knowing that he had to respect her boundaries. He had reached a dead end.

"Wait up, Goldie," he said, grabbing her hand as she passed. "If that's your final decision, I need to give you something." He delved into the pocket of his shorts and pulled out a small black device. "Take this."

"What is it?"

"It's a GPS tracker."

She shook her head, pushed his hand away. "You know I can't take that, Zeke. Christina would flip out if she knew you were trying to track me."

"It's only for emergencies," he said, continuing to hold it midair. "It's switched off right now, but if you find yourself in trouble, turn it on and I'll receive an alert on my cell phone. I'll be able to pinpoint your location immediately."

She looked at the tracker, seemingly of two minds.

"It's for emergencies only," he repeated. "If I can't be with you, this is the next best thing. If everything goes well, you'll never need it and you can destroy it."

She tentatively touched the plastic case. "I guess it can't hurt."

"I'm right at the other end of this button." He pointed to the switch. "Anytime."

She took the tracker and slipped it into the back pocket of her jeans. "I won't need it," she said confidently. "Nothing will go wrong."

"I know, but it gives me peace of mind."

With her index finger, she traced the line of his jaw before resting the tip on his stubbly chin. "You're a good guy, Zeke," she said. "I wish things had turned out differently for us."

"Me too."

She leaned forward, rising slightly onto her toes to kiss him on the lips, soft and firm and fleeting. When she pulled away, she was smiling, yet her eyes were moist.

"I don't have any more words left in me," she said. "So I'm hoping that the kiss says it all."

Goldie sat on the sofa, opposite Karl and Christina. Zeke sat by her side, occasionally rubbing her back or taking her hand, attentive to the end. He knew she was anxious and was doing his best to calm her nerves.

Her transport vehicle was late.

"I'm sorry about this, Goldie," Christina said, entering the room, cell in hand. "Your car appears to have been involved in an accident, so a replacement has been sourced."

Goldie stood. "An accident?" This didn't sound good. "What kind of accident?"

"I'm not sure of the details, but these kinds of things do sometimes happen, so let's not assume it's a bad sign."

Goldie exchanged a glance with Zeke, an unspoken worry passing between them. Christina clearly noticed their anxiety.

"Strange things happen in a heat wave," she said. "People act far crazier than they usually would and it's well-known that accidents increase along with the temperature."

"With your permission, ma'am," Zeke said, "I'd like to step in and transport Goldie myself. I have a bad feeling about this."

"That won't be necessary, Agent Miller," Christina replied. "The replacement vehicle should be here in just a few minutes."

Goldie tightly gripped Zeke's hand and suddenly felt the same bad feeling that he did.

"Actually," she said, "perhaps it wouldn't be such a bad idea if Zeke drove me to the safe house. We can trust him, right?"

Zeke gave her fingers a squeeze and smiled. This short delay had chipped away at her resolve and allowed Zeke's kindness to infiltrate her psyche. She had been imagining how happy they might be together if she took a chance. She was on the verge of cracking.

"Are you saying that you'd like Zeke to be assigned to your protection team?" Karl asked. "Because you were pretty certain that you didn't want him with you."

Her mind was torn. "I'm not sure. I think…" She glanced at him. "I think it might work, if Zeke is still open to the idea."

"Of course I am," he said, his eyes opening wide. "I'm always open to the idea of being with you."

Christina stood up as car headlights illuminated the darkened room and her radio crackled to life. "The car's here, and I think it's a little late to be changing the arrangements for the safe house."

Zeke held up a hand in protest. "I appreciate that we're asking you to break with formal procedures, but Goldie's life is about to be turned upside down. Surely you can make an allowance this one time?"

Christina unclipped her radio and spoke into it, confirming that an agent was ready for transportation. Then she looked between Goldie and Zeke and sighed.

"I don't know," she said finally. "I like to do things by the book, and we've made no arrangements for Zeke to be assigned to the case."

"Please," Zeke said. "Goldie has no one."

A shout rose from the hallway. It was Garth.

"I can't find Mrs. Volto," he called. "She's gone. Willy too."

Goldie's heart lurched. Had they been kidnapped? Or come to harm? "Have you searched the house?" she asked. "Everywhere?"

Garth came into the room, breathless and red cheeked. "There's a ladder propped up against the security fence out back," he said.

"And the barbed wire has been cut. They must've climbed over."

"But why?" Christina asked. "Mrs. Volto isn't under house arrest. If she wanted to go out, we'd have sent an agent to accompany her." She looked at the four faces in the room in confusion. "What's going on? Why would a heavily pregnant woman climb a ladder instead of leaving via the front door?"

"I don't know," Karl said, taking Goldie by the upper arm and leading her to the door. "But let's get Goldie out of here right now. This house definitely isn't safe anymore."

Goldie found herself being hustled toward the door, Karl's and Christina's radios springing to life. The atmosphere in the house, already dark, had turned sinister.

"Zeke," she called. "Can he come too?"

"I'm sorry, Goldie, but it's too late to make a change," Christina said. "You need to go right now."

"Can I say goodbye?" She held out her hand, just managing to graze Zeke's fingers as he followed her along the hall. "I just need a minute."

"We don't have a minute." Christina opened the door to reveal Officer Diaz waiting on the doorstep. "The officers will take good care of you, Goldie."

"I'm sorry for the delay, Agent Simmons," Officer Diaz said. "After your first car got into a traffic accident, Officer Moss and I stepped up to provide the transport instead."

"Let's get you in the car, Goldie," Christina said, leading her out into the still and balmy evening. "Officer Diaz will take you to an unmarked vehicle that's waiting for you at a highway rest stop. We're making sure you can't be tracked."

"Hold on!" Zeke was right behind them. "Can't you give us some time to say good-bye?"

Christina was in no mood to delay the proceedings any longer. "Mrs. Volto and Willy have vanished, the first transport vehicle got into an accident and there's no power in the house. Pardon me for being a little spooked, but I'd like to get this done quickly." She opened the door of a patrol car in the driveway and Goldie found herself being manhandled inside. "There's another police vehicle following behind for extra reassurance, so you're well protected."

Christina closed the door and gave a tense smile.

"Wait!" Goldie placed her hand flat on the window, through which she could see Zeke standing on the pavement. "We just need a minute."

Christina tapped her hand on the roof of the car and Officer Diaz started up the engine, turning slowly on the large driveway.

"Don't worry, Agent Simmons," Officer Moss said from the passenger seat. "We'll take good care of you."

"But I just needed a minute." She began to cry. "I didn't even get to say goodbye."

Officer Diaz drove quickly through the open gates, and Goldie shifted in her seat to see Zeke standing by the front door, an expression of anguish on his face. He had wanted to come with her, had tried to persuade her that it was the right choice. And now that she finally felt ready to accept his love, she found she had left it too late.

She was well and truly on her own.

TEN

Zeke watched Goldie's car roll through the ornate driveway gates and turn onto the road. He continued to track her until the taillights were just a blur in the distance while he rubbed at his chest where a pain was building. Goldie had been on the verge of allowing him to go with her, but the sudden and unexpected disappearance of Mrs. Volto and Willy Murphy had spooked Christina and caused her to panic. Now she was searching the house once more with Garth, determined to find a clue to their whereabouts or why they vanished.

"Who's that?" Karl began walking down the driveway to where an officer stood guard at the gate. "A vehicle is trying to get inside."

A gleaming SUV had stopped at the gate and the officer drew his gun, warning the occupants to exit the vehicle. Both Zeke and Karl also drew their weapons, Zeke doubly concerned that this might be a distraction from an attempt to pursue Goldie's car.

"Don't shoot. Please don't shoot." A middle-aged man was exiting the vehicle, holding his arms aloft. "My wife is in the car. We're the new owners of this house."

Karl turned and looked at Zeke, his eyebrows dancing quizzically. "Did he say what I think he said?"

"Yes, sir." Zeke had to try to push all thoughts of Goldie aside, no matter how overwhelming they might be. "Apparently they think they own this house."

"Pat them down and let them through," Karl called to the officer. "The car stays out on the street." He kept his gun in hand while the officer searched the couple for weapons. "What on earth is gonna go wrong next?"

The officer gave the all-clear signal and Karl holstered his weapon, standing next to Zeke while the couple made their way along the driveway. Both dressed in casual summer clothes, they had an air of wealth about them, from the Rolex on the wrist of the man to the expensive honey-colored highlights on the woman. They were definitely Gladwyne style folks but almost certainly had made a mistake in believing they owned this particular home.

"Hi there." The man approached with a nervous wave of the hand. "Pardon the intrusion, but we're a little worried about the explosion that happened inside this house earlier this evening."

Karl narrowed his eyes. "How did you know it was an explosion?"

"We heard it clear as a bell," the woman interjected, wringing her hands while she scanned every part of the house. "And then we saw the smoke and the fire department and the mayhem." She pointed toward the end of the street. "We're staying with a friend just a block away while we wait for Mrs. Volto to vacate the house."

Karl shook his head. "What are you talking about?"

"This is ours," the woman said, pointing to the house. "Our new home."

Karl was struck dumb for a moment. "You own this house?"

"Of course," the woman replied. "We brought everything from our home in Lancaster and it's sitting in three moving trucks, just waiting to be taken inside tomorrow." She took a tentative step forward. "Is there much damage inside? Please tell me it's not too bad."

"Can you explain to me exactly what's

going on?" Karl asked. "Because I must be missing something."

"We bought this house," the man said, speaking slowly as if Karl were an imbecile. "We saw it advertised a few weeks ago and made an offer without even viewing it. These properties don't come available very often, so we knew we'd have to get in quick. And our friends tell us it's a beautiful period home, one of the best in Gladwyne."

"You purchased this house?" Karl repeated, seemingly unable to get his head around it. "From Mrs. Volto?"

"Yes," the woman replied a little impatiently. "She explained her situation and told us about the trial and the security around the house, so we agreed to wait until she was able to leave before completing the purchase. The cash payment went through this morning, and we signed the papers so we're now officially the new owners. Mrs. Volto said we could move in tomorrow, but after hearing the explosion, we wanted to come check everything was all right. After all, we paid a lot of money for this place."

Karl and Zeke stared at each other in disbelief.

"Were you not aware of this transaction?" the man asked. "You seem rather surprised."

"Yeah," Zeke said, with a scratch of his head. "We had no idea that Mrs. Volto was intending to sell. How could she sell the place without her husband's permission? Half of it belongs to him."

"Her husband's signature is on the paperwork too," the woman said, still scanning the house for signs of damage. "So it looks like he gave his permission." She laughed nervously. "Unless Mrs. Volto forged his signature on the papers."

Zeke considered this possibility. Just what was Mrs. Volto up to? "Do you know where she is?"

"No idea," the man said. "We've been trying to call her since the explosion, but her cell is switched off and her lawyer isn't picking up either. Is she not here?"

A seed of fear began to grow, watered by the words of this couple, who were now apparently the brand-new owners of Mrs. Volto's palatial home.

"Mrs. Volto has vanished," Zeke said. "And her house still contains all her furniture. I suggest you get yourself a lawyer and return in the morning with all your legal paperwork to show the FBI." He took Karl by the arm and led him a few feet away. "I don't like this, sir. Something's wrong. I mean *really* wrong. We need to check on Goldie."

"I agree," Karl said, unclipping his radio. "It seems too much of a coincidence that Louisa and Willy vanish right at the same time as Goldie goes into hiding."

Zeke heard Karl's radio crackle with voices, and he strained to hear what was being said. Meanwhile, the anxious couple in the driveway gave him facts and figures about their house purchase that he didn't care about at all. The only thing on his mind at that moment was Goldie. Was she safe? Could he reach her in time if she wasn't?

"The support car has lost the lead vehicle," Karl shouted, running toward the house, radio in hand. "And the first car didn't get into an accident. The tires were tampered with and it veered off the freeway into the woods. You're right, Zeke, something's gone wrong. I think Diaz might be our mole."

Zeke's stomach dropped away as he followed his boss to the front door. "Diaz? The officer who captured Marty Foster?"

"Yeah, but I also think he might have been the one who murdered him in his cell."

"We have to find Goldie." Zeke grabbed his keys from the hook in the hallway. "We'll take my car."

"We don't know where she is." Karl's voice was loud and panicked. "The GPS in the patrol car has been disabled. They've gone off-grid."

"No problem," Zeke said, tearing toward the garage, ignoring the shocked faces of the couple watching the drama unfold. "I gave her a tracker." Pulling out his cell phone, he was overjoyed to see that she had activated it only moments ago. "She'll be waiting for me to come for her."

Goldie slipped the black GPS tracker into the crack of the seat in the patrol car, praying that Zeke would find her, that he would be able to save her from the dramatic situation she had found herself in. Officer Diaz had suddenly sped up, taking sharp twists and turns on the streets, ignoring the protests of Officer Moss in the passenger seat.

He was clearly trying to lose the support vehicle on their rear. And one minute ago, he had succeeded. Now they were on a quiet road, which Goldie knew led to a disused warehouse a few miles outside the city.

"I told you to stop the car, Diaz," Officer Moss shouted for the umpteenth time. "I don't know what you're trying to do, but if you don't desist, I'll be placing you under arrest."

Officer Diaz slowed, pulled to the side of the road and turned to his colleague with a smile. Officer Moss realized too late that he was in danger, reaching for his weapon just a moment after Diaz reached for his. Calmly, and without word, Officer Diaz shot his colleague twice in the chest, causing him to cry out in shock and pain. Then Diaz leaned across the slumped body to open the door. Goldie screamed as the body of Officer Moss fell with a thud onto the sun-parched scrubland. She yanked at the handle of her door and pushed her shoulder against it, knowing it was futile. Her weapon had been destroyed by the bomb explosion, and she had not been issued a new one. She was at the mercy of the officer assigned to protect her.

"Please listen to me, Brandon," she said to him, as he pulled back onto the road. "That's your name, right? Brandon?"

"Don't try to make a connection with me, lady," he said, his eyes remaining straight ahead. "I've been working for the Mob for too long to let anybody talk me out of anything."

"I don't understand," she said. "I thought you were a good guy. You captured Marty Foster, didn't you?"

He laughed, loud and prolonged. "After I managed to get you outside using the dummy in the pool, I went into the hills to help Marty target you. I thought he could use a hand, considering you were managing to stay below the water for so long between breaths. But then the SWAT team turned up and caught me with him, so I had to pretend I'd just arrested him. What else could I do?" He shrugged. "Marty went along with it for a while, before he realized that I couldn't help him escape the charges. He wanted to cut a deal and spill his guts to Agent Phillips."

"So you murdered him?"

"It wasn't easy, I can tell you. Marty was a big guy, strong, and he fought like a horse."

Goldie put her head in her hands, thinking of Officer Moss lying on the ground, shown no respect or mercy by his ruthless colleague, cruelly eliminated just like Marty Foster.

"Did you let Marsha into the house?" she asked. "On the first day I arrived."

"Of course I did. I've been working for Mr. Volto for about eight years. He's a good man, and very discreet. I'm sorry to see him in jail because my money is drying up like a hot riverbed. Mr. Volto got a message to me saying that Marsha would be visiting Louisa for a little chat, and I needed to help her get inside. I cooked up some story about a big man overpowering me, but I let Marsha tie me up in the garage and wear my shirt." He shook his head. "I stole an FBI schedule from my boss's office, but I didn't know it was an old one, so Marsha got the name of your partner wrong. That was a stupid mistake. I should've been more careful."

"What did Marsha want to chat to Louisa about?" Goldie hoped that she might be able to make a connection through conversation. She just had to keep him talking. "It seems a little odd not to kill her and stop her from testifying, don't you think?"

"You think Mr. Volto is a total monster, don't you?" He took a sharp turn onto a dirt road and the car bumped and rattled. "Mr. Volto would never hurt his wife. He forgave her for turning on him, and all he ever wanted in return was news on the baby and some sonogram pictures. But Louisa gave him nothing. She cut him from her life like a piece of trash, and that hurt him badly. His unborn baby means everything to him."

Goldie could see that there was a deep bond between Brandon Diaz and Leonardo Volto, one that had kept the officer loyal for eight years. And continued to keep him loyal now.

"I guess you want to pocket that two-million-dollar reward," she said, wringing her hands. "But you'd better have an escape plan, because there's no going back after this, you know that, right?"

He eyeballed her through the rearview mirror. "I'm not the mastermind behind the plan to kill you," he said with a laugh. "I never was. I got Marsha into the house and I piloted the drone to spy on Louisa, but—"

She interrupted him. "That first drone was controlled by you?"

"Sure. Mr. Volto wanted to see his wife and her big baby belly, so I said I'd try to get him some footage. But that crummy agent went and spoiled it, so I didn't get anything at all. I hated to let Mr. Volto down like that."

"Did you pilot the second one?" she asked. "The one with the bomb?"

"Nah." He seemed to be happy to talk freely, to expose all his secrets, and she knew why—she was going to be killed. "I never wanted to kill you. That was all Willy's plan."

Goldie's stomach fell away, as if an elevator had just stopped abruptly. "Willy? All this time, it was Willy trying to kill me?"

Diaz laughed heartily, as if enjoying her shock. "Willy's a devious man. Why else do you think he's the Mafia's favorite lawyer? He wanted that two million bucks, and when he saw my drone spying on Louisa, it gave him an idea. Instead of killing you with a bullet, he thought he could do it with a bomb on a drone instead. Except it didn't really go according to plan because you just refuse to die, no matter what he tries."

"How do you know it was Willy trying to kill me? Did he tell you?"

"Aside from Mr. Volto, Willy's the only other person who knows I'm on the Mafia payroll. He guessed that Mr. Volto was using me to spy on his wife, so he decided to also retain my services to help him kill you." He whistled through his teeth. "That man will do anything for money, I can tell you."

The road became bumpier and Goldie reached up to hold the handle above her head, being jerked in every direction.

"Willy must've realized that you let Marsha into the house," she said. "He knew you were placing Louisa in danger, and he did nothing about it."

"I already told you that Mr. Volto would never hurt his wife." Diaz's voice contained a note of anger. "He just wanted updates on her pregnancy. And why would Willy care about Louisa anyway? He just cares about money."

She leaned forward. "Willy and Louisa are having an affair. I caught them together."

Diaz flicked his eyes between the road and

Goldie. "You're a liar," he said finally. "Just trying to stir things up."

"I'm not lying," she protested, hoping that this piece of information would buy her some time. "Willy was terrified that Mr. Volto would find out about their affair and have them both killed. That's why the drone scared him so much. Your camera almost caught them in bed together."

"Really?" Diaz's interest was piqued. "Are you serious?"

"I'm telling the truth," she said. "How do you think Mr. Volto would feel if he knew that his pregnant wife was having a relationship with a crooked lawyer? It would certainly make him question whether the baby is his. And you wouldn't want to help Willy claim the reward money when he's betrayed your boss, right?"

Diaz narrowed his eyes. "That baby is Mr. Volto's," he said emphatically. "The only reason I'm doing this is so I can deliver you to Willy and Mrs. Volto. Then we split the reward money, and I disappear with Mrs. Volto to help take care of the baby on behalf of her husband. I promised to supply him with regular pictures and updates on the little guy's progress." He tapped the side of his nose. "Mr. Volto also wants me to keep an eye on his wife if you know what I mean. Sure, she betrayed him, but she's the mother of his child and if she does right by the kid, he won't hurt her. He doesn't want her running around with other men, so I'll make sure she stays faithful."

This news about Mrs. Volto's involvement was even more devastating than the news she had heard already. "Mrs. Volto is part of this?" She watched the industrial warehouse come into view, huge, gray and derelict, well-known in law enforcement circles as a favorite place for drug dealers to complete transactions. "I thought we were friends."

Diaz laughed again. "Boy, you really are slow on the uptake, aren't you? Mrs. Volto broke the air-conditioning, she enticed you outside by sitting by the pool late at night, she planted the bomb in your room and she even tried to get the details of your next safe house. She's as crafty as her husband, which is why he loves her so much." He shook his head with a chuckle. "A woman like Louisa would never be romantic with Willy Murphy. That's a crazy idea, and I ain't falling for it. They're just business partners and nothing more."

"They're more than business partners. They share everything, including a bed. And they've fooled you into cooperating with them."

"That's enough!" Diaz shouted. "Willy warned me you'd try to pull the wool over my eyes, but he's one step ahead. He respects Mrs. Volto, and her only involvement with him has been to help him implement the plan to kill you."

Goldie began to panic as the car stopped outside the vast and imposing building. "Why would Mrs. Volto need to disappear if she's got nothing to hide?" she asked quickly. "Why doesn't she stay in Gladwyne and raise the child there?"

"Because she wants to go someplace nobody knows her." He opened his door, stepped out and walked around the car. "We're going to Europe. Mr. Volto agreed to sell the house, and Mrs. Volto transferred all her money overseas." He grabbed Goldie by the hair and dragged her onto the dusty ground. "With the split two-million-dollar reward, we'll have more than enough to give the baby a chance of a good life."

She screamed as he dragged her along the ground by her red curls, her heels kicking up hot earth. "What if I'm right? What if the baby is Willy's? You'd be doing all of this for nothing."

"Shut up. You talk too much."

Officer Diaz unceremoniously yanked her up several cast-iron steps and into the building, where he threw her onto the concrete floor.

"Hello, Goldie." Mrs. Volto was standing over her. "I've been waiting for you."

Zeke raced along the dirt road, his headlights illuminating the dark road while Karl navigated in the passenger seat. He was desperate to reach Goldie, praying he wouldn't be too late.

"We're almost there," Karl said, pointing to an abandoned and derelict warehouse up ahead. "Backup won't be here for at least five or six minutes, so we'll have to go in alone. You okay with that Zeke?"

"Absolutely, sir," he replied, killing the lights before stopping the vehicle next to Officer Diaz's parked patrol car. "I'm not wasting a second." He pulled his gun from its holster. "You ready?"

"Don't let your heart rule your head," Karl said. "You're emotionally involved in this, so you need to remember to keep calm."

"I am calm, sir." Zeke's chest was pounding like a freight train, but he was a master at maintaining a cool facade. "I won't do anything to jeopardize Goldie's life, I can assure you of that."

He exited the car, looking up at the huge building jutting into the starlit sky, knowing that Goldie was somewhere inside. Walking silently and quickly across the baked ground, he stopped, raised a hand to halt Karl in his tracks and brought a finger to his lips. Voices were floating from somewhere inside the decrepit building, close by, both male and female. And one of them was Mrs. Volto's.

Zeke pointed to the entrance, indicating he was going inside, and Karl nodded. They approached with caution, flattening their backs against the side of the building before sliding around the wall, making their way to the sounds of activity, of anger and raised voices.

"We had a deal!" Officer Diaz was shouting. "We agreed that I'd travel with you to Europe. I promised Mr. Volto that I'd take care of his child."

"You let Marsha into my home!" Mrs. Volto yelled in response. "She almost killed me, and it's your fault. Why should I ever trust you?"

"Let's all calm down and take a moment to breathe." This was Willy's soft and measured tone. "Officer Diaz had no idea what he was doing, Louisa. He thought he was simply helping Leonardo check on his baby. He doesn't know that there *is* no baby."

"What do you mean?" Officer Diaz was now confused, with a note of fear in his voice. "There's no baby?"

Zeke reached the edge of a huge room, most likely where factory machinery would've once been housed, but which was now crumbling and moldy. He peeked around the wall to see Goldie standing in the center of the room, Officer Diaz next to her. A few feet away were Willy and Mrs. Volto, both holding handguns, their figures dimly lit by the moonlight shining through a glassless window. Zeke steadied himself, ready to launch into action. But first, with Goldie in no imminent danger, he watched and listened, waiting for an opportune moment.

Mrs. Volto smiled, slipped a hand beneath the shoulder of her dress and seemed to unclip something. As soon as she repeated the process with the other shoulder, a large false belly fell from her skirt and landed with a thud on the concrete, where it lay in an oddly-shaped heap. Then Mrs. Volto smoothed the fabric of her dress, laughing.

"Look, Willy," she said scornfully. "I just gave birth."

Officer Diaz appeared to be struck dumb

as he stared at the beige lump on the ground. Finally, it was Goldie who spoke, her voice wavering.

"You lied about your baby," she said. "It was never real."

Mrs. Volto pointed to the false belly. "That was the only thing keeping me alive until I could escape," she spat. "As long as I was the mother of Leonardo's child, he would never hurt me. But he wanted updates and sonogram pictures and doctor's reports, and I couldn't provide them."

Now Officer Diaz was catching up. "That's why he sent Marsha."

"As soon as Marsha started asking questions, she knew I was hiding something," Mrs. Volto said. "She pushed me against the wall, discovered the false belly and went crazy. If she'd managed to report back to Leonardo, I'd have been dead by sundown." She walked a little way along the concrete, her heels echoing in the dark and open space. "But every cloud has a silver lining, and now Goldie is going to provide me with an extra two million dollars for my escape fund."

"I thought we were friends, Louisa," Goldie said in a small voice. "I trusted you."

"Well, then, you're a fool," she shot back. "Because I was only doing what was necessary to get you where I wanted you. You're a member of law enforcement, and that makes you scum as far as I'm concerned."

Zeke brought his gun to shoulder height. He needed to strike soon.

"Did you just say you're keeping the two million dollars?" Officer Diaz asked. "Willy and I agreed to share the reward money. Even if there is no baby, I can't go back to my old life now. We made a deal."

"I lied," Willy said matter-of-factly. "Because Louisa and I need that money to make a life together, far away from Leonardo and his cronies and anyone else who can hurt us."

Officer Diaz turned to Goldie, open-mouthed. "You were right," he said. "They're together. They double-crossed me."

"Of course they did," Goldie said. "They don't care about anybody but themselves."

Zeke watched as Goldie then turned to Mrs. Volto. "I can't believe I was ever concerned for you, Louisa. You're despicable."

Mrs. Volto's laugh echoed off the concrete walls, bouncing back at them. "I may be despicable but I'm also very rich, and you're about to make me two million dollars richer." She looked across at Willy. "Kill Diaz first. Then the agent."

Officer Diaz wasted no time in reaching

for his weapon in response to the command, but he was too slow. Zeke leaped out from behind the wall and ran toward Goldie just as a bullet left Willy's gun. Officer Diaz yelled out in shock and pain before crumpling to the ground, clutching his chest, blood seeping through his fingers. Goldie screamed, turned to flee and ran straight into Zeke's arms, fighting him at first, until realizing that he was her safety. She clung to him as he took her off her feet, swung her around and positioned her body behind him. Then he raised his gun toward Willy and Mrs. Volto, noticing Karl in his peripheral vision edging his way into the hall.

"It's all over, Mrs. Volto," he said, his feet planted firmly in front of Goldie. "If you give yourself up now, you stand a chance of making it out of here alive."

Both Willy's and Mrs. Volto's weapons were raised in response to the unexpected appearance of two FBI agents riding roughshod over their perfect plan of escape.

"If you give us Goldie, we'll let you live," Willy said, enunciating carefully. "She's the only thing we want."

"No deal," Zeke said, backing slowly toward the exit, gently pushing Goldie. "I'd rather die."

"He's in love with her, stupid," Mrs. Volto hissed to Willy. "He'd never give her up."

"He would if I shot him." Willy smiled, aiming his weapon. "Should I go for the head or the chest?"

"Stop!" Karl yelled from his position at the back of the atrium. "You take one shot and you die."

"Nobody else has to die," Willy yelled back. "All we want is Goldie. Just give her to us, and we'll leave without any trouble."

Zeke felt Goldie tuck her fingers into the belt on his jeans and cling on tight, her breathing rapid and shallow. If he needed to sacrifice his life for her, he would do it gladly.

"It's okay," he said to her quietly. "I'm not going anywhere. I'm in this for the long haul, all the way to the end."

"We're not making any deals with you, Willy," Karl called. "Backup is almost here. Can you hear the sirens?"

Willy lifted an ear to the air, the faint sound of police sirens ringing in the distance. "Don't be a hero, Agent Miller," he said to Zeke. "Be sensible and step aside."

"I already told you, Willy," Mrs. Volto said, beginning to retreat to an exit on the opposite side of the hall. "He's in love with her. He'd rather die than let us have her." She pulled on

Willy's sleeve. "Come on, we gotta go. There isn't much time to get to our plane."

Willy resisted. "I want that two million dollars."

"We already have enough." Mrs. Volto was panicking, her eyes darting to the window to try to catch a glimpse of the approaching cars. "Let it go."

"Think of the difference that two million dollars would make to us, Louisa," he said. "Europe is expensive and we want to live the high life, right?"

"Listen to her, Willy," Zeke said, the combined heat and tension causing sweat to pour down his temples. "You'll never get to Goldie because I won't let you."

Willy narrowed his eyes, his impatience apparently giving way to anger. He squeezed the trigger, and Zeke felt a searing pain rip through his shoulder as his body jerked backward with the force of the bullet.

Goldie shrieked and held out both hands to steady Zeke as his back arched with a sudden and violent jolt. He cried out in pain, yet he didn't release his weapon. He took aim and fired in immediate response, narrowly missing Willy, who dived to the floor and rolled on the concrete, coming to rest behind an old plywood counter. Mrs. Volto shouted, cursing angrily while running to the exit on the opposite side of the hall.

"You're on your own, Willy," she screamed. "I have a plane to catch."

"We need to take cover," Zeke said, pulling Goldie toward a pile of rubble in the corner. "Quickly." He yelled to Karl, "Go get Mrs. Volto before she escapes."

"You're hurt," Goldie said, as she and Zeke scrambled behind a high mound of broken bricks. "Give me the gun and I'll take over."

"Let me do this for you," he said, gritting his teeth against the pain. "If I hold off Willy, it'll give you time to climb through that window." He pointed to a frame in the wall, its glass long smashed into pieces and fallen to the floor. "I'll count to three and you run, okay?"

There must be a better way, but Goldie couldn't think clearly or breathe properly or even stand firmly.

"No, Zeke," she said. "You've already been shot once and I'm guessing you have no spare ammo once your bullets are gone."

"Go!" he urged. "On three." He made a fist and started to count down by extending his fingers one by one. "Three...two..."

She jumped up on one, just as the bullets

began to fly. Launching herself onto the ledge of the empty window frame, she swung her legs over the side, ready to leap. But something was terribly wrong. The drop was at least forty feet, far more than she'd anticipated. One half of this factory was facing a steep hillside, unseen from the front. There was no way she'd be able to survive this descent. Hauling herself back over the ledge, she made a break for the door. But then a bullet cracked into the floor beside her and she stopped in her tracks, vulnerable and exposed. The gunfire had ceased, leaving a tinny ringing in her ears, one that hummed over the sounds of the sirens still some distance away.

"Stop right there!" Willy was striding toward her, his gun held in a straight arm. In his other hand, he held a cell phone, apparently recording the scene before him. "This should be all the evidence I need to get that money."

She squeezed her eyes tightly shut, waiting for the moment to come, but what she felt instead was Zeke's back pressed against her torso, his arms stretched out to the side as if trying to shield every inch of her body. She guessed that he was out of ammo.

"Step aside, Agent Miller." Willy was clearly anxious, continually glancing at the exit. "I'm in rather a hurry, but contrary to what you might believe, I don't like to kill innocent people. I'll let you live if you co-operate."

"Goldie's innocent," Zeke said, not missing a beat. "She did nothing wrong."

Willy considered that for a second. "You're always ready with a smart answer, aren't you?" He pointed his gun at Zeke's head. "Was Louisa right? Would you die for her?"

"Without a doubt."

Willy raised his eyebrows. "As you wish."

Goldie wrapped her arms around Zeke's waist and rested her cheek on his muscled back, strangely thankful that they would be dying together. It somehow felt right, exactly as it was meant to be.

"I love you," she whispered. "I always did."

When the bullet sounded, she waited for Zeke's body to fall, yet he remained upright and steadfast. The body to fall was Willy's, crumpling downward, legs first, like a collapsing tower. And behind Willy was Karl, standing in the wide doorway, a faint wisp of smoke curling from the barrel of his gun. He rushed toward Willy, his weapon continually trained on the prone figure lying on the filthy concrete.

"Is he dead?" Zeke asked.

"He's dead," Karl confirmed, crouching over the body. "It's a good thing I was able to come back so quick. Mrs. Volto sped out of here like a freight train and lost control of the car on the dirt road. She's at the bottom of a ravine about a half mile away. I'll go radio for help to get her, but I don't think she'll have survived." He patted Zeke's uninjured shoulder. "Good job, Agent Miller. I'm proud of you."

"I can't thank you enough, sir," Zeke said. "I'm glad you had my back."

"And you had Agent Simmons's back from what I saw," Karl said with a smile. "That was an honorable thing you did for her." He began to walk to the exit. "You two make an awesome team."

Zeke placed a hand over Goldie's, which was rested around his waist, and gently rubbed her fingers. Meanwhile, she breathed into the cotton of his shirt against his back, steadying her heart, calming her nerves and reminding herself that she was alive. And so was Zeke. This was a brand-new start for them.

"Are you okay?" she asked. "That was pretty terrifying, huh?"

He turned around, holding his shoulder tight to his body and clamping his jaw

with the pain. After glancing at the blood-
ied bodies on the ground, he led her away
from the sight, toward a stone pillar in the
corner, which would obscure the view. What
had happened there today would undoubtedly
leave its mark on both of them but, for now,
Zeke was trying to minimize the trauma, and
she adored him for his tenderness.

"Thank you," she said, as they stood just
inches apart. "I can't believe what you just
did for me."

"It was a no-brainer. I was never going to
leave you."

"But staying with me could've involved
taking a bullet to the head."

He stared at her. "I know."

"You'd have sacrificed yourself?"

"Of course." He placed a palm against her
cheek, warm and soft. "When I said I was in
this all the way to the end, I meant it. It was
my choice, right? Just like it's my choice to
want to leave everything behind and be with
you."

She searched his face, looking for any hint
of indecision, a reason to reject his offer. She
found nothing but sincerity and hope.

"Are you sure?" she asked. "You have to
be sure, Zeke."

"I love you, Goldie. I've always loved you. Don't make me live without you."

She blinked rapidly, not wanting to ruin this moment by crying.

"We might end up on a dusty plain in Idaho."

"That's okay by me. I love potatoes." He leaned forward and kissed her full on the mouth. "But I love you more."

"I love you too."

He took her hand, squeezed it tight. "Let's go. We've got a whole new life to plan."

EPILOGUE

Goldie stood on a stepladder, hanging new drapes in a cozy cabin on the banks of the Columbia River. Her beautiful home was in the small town of Hood River, Oregon, a place she and Zeke had chosen after weeks of discussion and deliberation. They had both fallen in love with the cabin as soon as they'd laid eyes on it, with its wooden jetty, tethered boat and leafy yard, all set against the breathtaking backdrop of a huge, snowy mountain. It couldn't have been any more perfect.

"Hey." Zeke came through the door, carrying logs for the fire, stocking up for the winter months ahead. He saw her on the ladder, dropped the logs and rushed forward. "What are you doing up there?" He lifted her from the step and lowered her to the floor. "You shouldn't be doing things like that in your condition."

She laughed. "I'm pregnant, not an invalid."

He placed a protective hand on her stomach. "And you only have one month to go, so let me hang the drapes and do all the heavy work, okay?"

"You have a job to do," she said, straightening the collar on his plaid shirt.

"I can take a little time off and let the mechanics take care of things for a while." He gathered her into his arms. "That's one of the perks of being the boss, right?"

She smiled. Zeke had used the proceeds from the sale of his apartment in New York to buy a local car-repair shop, committing himself to learning how to fix all manner of vehicles. In little more than a year, the business was thriving, and he had managed to employ three staff members, creating a secure financial situation that allowed Goldie to take some well needed time off, to rest and recuperate and heal emotionally. Finding a great church had helped in that process, and they'd become part of a large church family, where God had provided wonderful friends and joyful worship.

"It's Christmas in six weeks' time," she said, looking down at her swollen belly. "If this little guy holds on, we could have a holiday baby."

"Great. We'll choose the name Noel for a boy and Holly for a girl."

"You know what we agreed," she said with a laugh. "Ezekiel for a boy and Marigold for a girl."

He smiled at her. "For somebody who always hated her name, I'm amazed you want to continue that particular tradition."

Her smiled faded a little. "We're not Marigold and Zeke anymore, and I kind of want our names to live on somehow."

The whole process of changing identities had been arduous, only made bearable by the fact that Zeke was at her side. His upbeat and positive nature had kept her sane, made her laugh, allowed her to see the blessings in everything and given her hope for the future. He had never once complained, not even in cold weather when his shoulder injury caused stiffness and pain. He had been her rock.

"Are you okay?" Zeke asked, noticing her waning smile. "You like it here in Hood River, right?"

"I love it here," she replied. "It's the best place in the world, but sometimes it's still hard to adjust to being a different person."

He cupped her cheek with his hand. "I know, but we were told that it's a long process." Kissing her nose, he added, "And as long as we have each other, we can face anything, right?"

Her smile now returned with force. "Absolutely. I don't know what I'd do without you, Jon." She giggled. Even now, after almost two years in the program, she couldn't say Zeke's new name without a laugh or a frown. "After everything we've been through together, I think we might be the strongest couple in the world."

"Without a doubt," he replied, lacing his fingers through hers. "Unbreakable."

She suddenly felt the baby kick, a tiny hand or foot knocking on her belly as if asking to come out. She guided Zeke's hand to the spot and held it there while they gazed at each other, reveling in the new life they had created.

"This little one is ready to say hello," Zeke said. "I can't wait to meet him." He checked himself. "Or her."

"I've been thinking," she said. "We could ask the Marshals to arrange a meeting with your parents around the time of the birth. They'd want to meet the baby as soon as possible, right?"

While Goldie truly adored her life with Zeke, she still needed to ensure he retained a link with his family. Life in the Witness

Protection Program allowed for these occasional visits, always carefully managed by the US Marshals to ensure secrecy was maintained. Zeke's parents had even been at their wedding, the only guests besides Christina, Karl and Goldie's sister, to watch them make a promise to love each other for the rest of their lives. Their new names had taken some getting used to for everybody concerned, but that became easier as time passed. Zeke Miller and Goldie Simmons were now firmly in the past. They were now Jonathan and Mary Freemont, newlyweds from Los Angeles, seeking a quiet and peaceful life in Hood River to raise a family. Along with their new identities came a sense of freedom and a clean slate upon which they could write a new story.

"I'll get in touch with the Marshals through the secure channels and see what they can set up during the holidays." He held her close. "Are you sure you want to continue to see my parents after what they did to keep us apart years ago?"

"They did what they thought was best," she said. "We all want to do the right thing for our children, and I don't hold a grudge. After all, things worked out well for us in the end, didn't they?"

"They sure did."

"I can't believe I ever doubted that God had it all under control," she said. "He answered my prayer, just twenty-one years after I first asked it."

"I guess that's how He teaches us patience."

Goldie smiled and rested her face on Zeke's chest, breathing in his car-grease scent. He would always be Zeke to her, even though she now called him Jon. He would always be her first love, the fresh-faced boy who goofed around and made her crease up with laughter. She had adored him then just as much as she adored him now.

His heart was beating rhythmically beneath her ear, as steady and dependable as his character.

"No regrets?" she asked, pulling away to look into his face.

"None at all," he said, kissing her forehead. "My place is with you, wherever that may be."

"I love you, Mr. Freemont," she said. "Always."

"Ditto, Mrs. Freemont. Thank you for making me the happiest man alive."

* * * * *

*If you enjoyed this story, be sure to pick up
Elisabeth Rees's previous book,*
Safe House Under Fire, *which introduces
Goldie and features her FBI partner,
David McQueen.*

*Available now from
Love Inspired Suspense!*

Dear Reader,

Sometimes, having faith can be difficult. It isn't always plain sailing, and there are periods when we might struggle to remember that we are important to God. In Goldie, I tried to create a character who carries a lot of pain and anger, and whose faith hangs by a thread as a consequence.

It is tempting to tell people like Goldie how to rebuild their faith, because we might think we know the answers—pray more, worry less, let go of resentment, listen to God, read your Bible. This is all good advice, but very difficult for people to digest when they are in a pit of despair.

Zeke couldn't comprehend how or why Goldie was struggling to connect with God, because his faith was unshakable. He initially didn't understand that she simply wanted to be loved and supported, and not judged for being spiritually weak. When people are broken, our job is not to fix them but to sit with them in their brokenness until they are ready to resume their walk of faith once again.

Zeke and Goldie eventually found the path that God wanted them to take, but it wasn't easy, and they suffered greatly before finding happiness. If you are struggling right now, keep going. Because you are one of God's stories, and they always end with a happy-ever-after.

Blessings,
Elisabeth

Get 4 FREE REWARDS!

We'll send you 2 FREE Books plus 2 FREE Mystery Gifts.

Love Inspired books feature uplifting stories where faith helps guide you through life's challenges and discover the promise of a new beginning.

FREE
Value Over
$20

YES! Please send me 2 FREE Love Inspired Romance novels and my 2 FREE mystery gifts (gifts are worth about $10 retail). After receiving them, if I don't wish to receive any more books, I can return the shipping statement marked "cancel." If I don't cancel, I will receive 6 brand-new novels every month and be billed just $5.24 each for the regular-print edition or $5.99 each for the larger-print edition in the U.S., or $5.74 each for the regular-print edition or $6.24 each for the larger-print edition in Canada. That's a savings of at least 13% off the cover price. It's quite a bargain! Shipping and handling is just 50¢ per book in the U.S. and $1.25 per book in Canada.* I understand that accepting the 2 free books and gifts places me under no obligation to buy anything. I can always return a shipment and cancel at any time. The free books and gifts are mine to keep no matter what I decide.

Choose one: ☐ **Love Inspired Romance Regular-Print** (105/305 IDN GNWC)   ☐ **Love Inspired Romance Larger-Print** (122/322 IDN GNWC)

Name (please print)

Address   Apt. #

City   State/Province   Zip/Postal Code

Email: Please check this box ☐ if you would like to receive newsletters and promotional emails from Harlequin Enterprises ULC and its affiliates. You can unsubscribe anytime.

> Mail to the **Reader Service:**
> **IN U.S.A.:** P.O. Box 1341, Buffalo, NY 14240-8531
> **IN CANADA:** P.O. Box 603, Fort Erie, Ontario L2A 5X3

Want to try 2 free books from another series? Call 1-800-873-8635 or visit www.ReaderService.com.

*Terms and prices subject to change without notice. Prices do not include sales taxes, which will be charged (if applicable) based on your state or country of residence. Canadian residents will be charged applicable taxes. Offer not valid in Quebec. This offer is limited to one order per household. Books received may not be as shown. Not valid for current subscribers to Love Inspired Romance books. All orders subject to approval. Credit or debit balances in a customer's account(s) may be offset by any other outstanding balance owed by or to the customer. Please allow 4 to 6 weeks for delivery. Offer available while quantities last.

Your Privacy—Your information is being collected by Harlequin Enterprises ULC, operating as Reader Service. For a complete summary of the information we collect, how we use this information and to whom it is disclosed, please visit our privacy notice located at corporate.harlequin.com/privacy-notice. From time to time we may also exchange your personal information with reputable third parties. If you wish to opt out of this sharing of your personal information, please visit readerservice.com/consumerschoice or call 1-800-873-8635. **Notice to California Residents**—Under California law, you have specific rights to control and access your data. For more information on these rights and how to exercise them, visit corporate.harlequin.com/california-privacy.

LI20R2